Enjoy every exci... _ ... _ , ... _ ,

The Wright Cousin Adventures
The Treasure of the Lost Mine
Desert Jeepers
The Secret of the Lost City
The Case of the Missing Princess
Secret Agents Don't Like Broccoli
The Great Submarine Adventure
Take to the Skies
The Wright Cousins Fly Again!
Reach for the Stars
The Sword of Sutherlee
The Secret of Trifid Castle
The Clue in the Missing Plane
The Wright Disguise
The Mystery of Treasure Bay
The Secret of the Sunken Ship
Wright Cousin Adventures Trilogy Sets 1-5

The Wright Cousin Adventures Cookbooks
#1 Fun Cookbook: Sweet Treats that bring a Happy Smile!

Additional Books
Rheebakken 2: Last Stand for Freedom
Strength of the Mountains: A Wilderness Survival Adventure
The Hat, George Washington, and Me!

For all the adventures, visit **GregoryOSmith.com**

"Kimberly," said Jonathan, "how did that smiley face get on the front cover of our book?"

"What?" said Kimberly. "Where?"

The CLUE in the
MISSING PLANE

The CLUE in the
MISSING PLANE

Gregory O. Smith

Dedication

To those who face big challenges and keep on going, trying to make things better and right, and to my three patient editors: Lisa Smith, Anne Smith, and Dorothy Smith.

Author's Note

Years ago, our family went to visit some lava tubes in Idaho. The ground surface was hot and dry, but as we descended into the earth, we discovered water and bright green moss. The air in the old lava tube was cooler. It was like a whole different world down there. These particular tubes had ice in them year-round. One section was so constricted with ice that we had to lay down on our backs and push ourselves along to go further into the tube. The jagged rock ceiling of the tube was just inches above our noses. Further back into the tube, it opened up again. We finally came to a part which was totally blocked with ice. Someone had carved notches in the ice so we could climb up to the top of it and slide down a thirty-foot long chute. We enjoyed sliding down it over and over again. Boy, was it fast!

In this book, the Wright cousins have a similar experience, except theirs might be quite a bit warmer. Will they find hot lava like Tim thinks they will? Can the Wrights discover the secret of the missing plane before it is too late?

Strap on your snow boots and get set for fun as the Wright cousins search for THE CLUE IN THE MISSING PLANE!

~ Gregory O. Smith

CHAPTER 1

The Flight

Snow was falling fiercely now. It was early afternoon. The Wright cousins had been in the air for two hours. They were flying over the mountains of southeastern Gütenberg in a twin-engine, turboprop passenger plane. Jonathan Wright was in the pilot's seat, Robert, his cousin, was co-pilot.

"The blizzard's getting worse," said Jonathan. "I can't see a thing."

"We've still got three hundred miles to go," Robert replied, looking out the window into the snowy daylight. "We're going to have to do it all by instrument if it doesn't let up. Why are we doing this flight in this terrible weather anyways?"

"The officer on the phone said this plane was needed at Kalisbehr. They also wanted us 'non-military personnel' off their air force base."

"You'd think they'd be nicer to us," said Robert. "After all we did to help their country at Pallin. If we didn't care about the Straunsees, we'd be out of here right now. By the way, why didn't Katrina and her sisters board the plane with us?"

"I don't think the officer wanted to tell his commander-in-chief, King Straunsee, that his daughters weren't welcome at the base," Jonathan replied.

"But they could have at least let us say good-bye to them," said Robert.

"They were clear on the other side of the base," said Jonathan, shaking his head. "But I know what you mean. With Gütenberg on the brink of war, they should have let us fly Sarina and her sisters to a safer location. Robert, this weather's getting crazy, see if you can find any closer airports."

"Okay," Robert replied. "I'll pull up the electronic charts."

"While you're doing that, I'm going to call in for some help," said Jonathan, switching to the radio. "Air control, this is Charlie-delta-foxtrot-two-five, over."

The plane the cousins were flying in was a civilian model, but it had been upgraded with military-type navigation equipment. It even had IFF—International Friend or Foe—aircraft recognition electronics.

"Air control, this is Charlie-delta-foxtrot-two-five, over. We are caught in a blizzard. We could use some navigational assistance. Over." Jonathan turned up the receiver's volume. There was nothing but static. "Air traffic control, this is Charlie-delta-foxtrot-two-five. Requesting help. Over."

"Jonathan," said Robert, looking at the screen, "somebody's following us."

"What do you mean?"

"We've got something on our tail and according to the IFF it's not friendly," Robert replied. "Look, there's a second one."

Jonathan scanned the electronics, "How long have they been there?"

"I don't know. At first, I thought it was just radar noise from the storm," Robert said.

"Bad time to be trailed by someone," Jonathan said. "Gütenberg could be engulfed in war at any moment and I don't want us to be the first casualties."

Jonathan spoke into his microphone to the other cousins in the plane's passenger compartment, "We've got somebody trailing us. We don't know who they are. Make sure your seatbelts are on tight, we may have to take evasive action."

"In this storm?" Kimberly called forward. "Jonathan, what are we going to do?"

"We'll just sit down and hold on tight," Lindy said from the seat beside her.

"Robert, punch in the TFR," said Jonathan.

"Okay, but it's going to make Kimberly airsick again," Robert replied.

"I hope not," said Jonathan, running up the engine throttles. "Kimberly, have you got your plastic bag?"

"Yes," Kimberly replied. "Tim just gave me one. But please tell me I won't have to use it."

"Just hang on and keep smiling," Jonathan replied.

Robert switched on the TFR—Terrain-following radar. An air force pilot had instructed him how to use it before they took off. TFR would allow their plane to hug the profile of the earth below, keeping them at a safe distance from the ground. They hoped it would make them drop below their pursuers' radar.

The cousins' plane nosed lower and began following the mountainous profile of the ground below.

"Jonathan, there are mountains down there," Kimberly called out worriedly. "And Tim's got homework to do. His handwriting is already too hard to read as it is."

"Thank you, thank you," said fourteen-year-old Tim Wright, seated beside her. "I'm practicing to become a doctor someday."

The cousins were now flying in a narrow canyon, the walls

were less than five-hundred feet from each side of the plane. They soon topped a mountain. As they did, a warning suddenly appeared on the instrument panel. They were back in radar range and had just been "painted"—targeted—by someone's weapons system. They dove into the next valley, out of radar range, but not soon enough. An air-to-air missile was locked onto them, following them at an extremely high speed. It slammed into their left engine and blew it to pieces. Kimberly and Lindy screamed as parts of engine and propeller smashed into the fuselage.

Jonathan and Robert fought to stabilize the plane. Smoke and fuel streamed from the left wing. The wing was shaking wildly and bending backward, threatening to collapse. Jonathan steered the plane downward. "Everybody hang on!" he shouted.

As they dropped below the ridges, the snowstorm suddenly let up. Jonathan spotted a flat area clear of brush and trees in the valley below and aimed for it. "This isn't going to be pretty," he called out. "Robert, get the landing gear down."

"We're descending too fast," said Robert.

"I know," Jonathan replied. "I'm doing everything I can, but that left wing isn't going to last much longer."

"The left gear won't lock," said Robert.

The ground was coming at them quickly now. The cousins in the passenger compartment gasped and held on tight as the stricken plane slammed down. The left landing gear collapsed and broke off, taking the left wing with it as the plane skidded across the icy ground. The right landing wheel also collapsed and the plane crunched onto its belly. A large snowbank loomed ahead. They smacked into it and plowed on through. The plane came to a grinding halt thirty feet from large rocks and trees.

"I can smell fuel!" shouted Lindy.

"Me too," said Jonathan, releasing his seatbelt harness and leaping into action. "Everybody grab your gear and get out of the plane," he yelled. "This thing could explode any second!"

The youths grabbed their backpacks, forced open the side door, and scrambled to get clear of the plane. Two fighter jets shrieked overhead and shot past them.

"They'll be back," Jonathan yelled, "run for it!"

Through the falling snow, the cousins saw a stone building in the distance and rushed toward it. The snow on the ground was now knee-high. Jonathan broke trail, lunging at times into even deeper drifts.

The Wright cousins were halfway to the building when the jets returned. Two large explosions rocked the area around the cousins' plane. The ground shook and trembled like an earthquake. The noise of the explosions echoed away, but the earth beneath the cousins' feet kept trembling.

Breaking through a tall snowdrift, the cousins found themselves on smooth ice. Behind them, they heard a high-pitched, eerie cracking noise working its way toward them. They were running on an ice-covered lake!

CHAPTER 2

Into the Storm

"Get to the building!" shouted Jonathan, redoubling his efforts as he plowed into another tall snowdrift.

Racing for high ground, the cousins could hear the sharp reports of the ice cracking behind them. "We're almost there," shouted Jonathan. There was a loud **CRACK!**

Jonathan and the others leapt for a tall bank of snow as the ice shattered and sunk under their feet. The cousins landed in a tangled heap just beyond the water's edge. They had reached the shore!

Their chests heaving, the Wrights crawled up the bank on their hands and knees to get away from the water's edge. The ice continued to crack. Something strange was happening: the ice appeared to be sinking in places.

"Is everybody okay?" called out Jonathan.

"Let's get out of here," said Kimberly, shivering.

The cousins scrambled up to the stone building. To their dismay, it was old and abandoned. It was missing its windows, doors, and roof. Its floor was buried under several feet of snow.

"So much for a warm reception," said Tim.

"There's another building over there," said Robert, pointing toward a distant structure. "Maybe it's in better shape."

The cousins made their way to the other structure but found it also roofless and filled with snow. As Lindy and Robert walked around the side of the old building, they spied a third building.

The youths, eager to find shelter from the blowing snow, hurried over to the next building. It appeared to be in much better condition than the others and still had its roof and windows in place. It was L-shaped. They hurried up to the front and peered inside one of the windows, rubbing the glass to clean it.

"Hey, there's a boat in there," said Lindy.

"And there's a wood-burning stove over in that corner," Robert said excitedly. "Now we just need some wood."

"A wood stove?" said Tim, shivering. "S-sounds good to me."

Robert tried the front door beside him; it was locked. He peered through the window again, spotted another door in the left wall, and slipped around to investigate it while the others were still looking in through the windows.

The second wooden door on the leeward side was slightly open. Robert glanced in; there was snow on the floor that had blown in through the crack.

"Hello," Robert called out. "Anybody home?" He pushed the door open more and stepped cautiously into the dimly lit room. "Hello?" he called out a second time. Still no answer. He closed the door behind him and walked over to the front door. He studied it for a moment, figured out how to unlock it, and tried to pull it open.

"Tim," Robert called out through the door, "push on the door. It's frozen in place."

Outside, Tim put his shoulder into the door and pushed as

hard as he could. Robert tugged on the inside. The door suddenly broke loose and Tim came flying through the doorway, spinning Robert around. They both landed on an old upside-down, dust covered rowboat with a resounding *THUNK!*

Jonathan, Kimberly, and Lindy rushed in to see if the boys were okay. Other than a sore elbow, Tim seemed fine.

Jonathan closed the door to stop more snow from blowing in and the youths looked over their new surroundings. The room looked as if it hadn't been occupied for over fifty years. In fact, there was a newspaper on the floor that proved that point.

"We can't just stay here without permission," said Kimberly.

"Kimberly, you can stay out there in the snow if you want to," said Jonathan, "but I don't want to freeze to death."

"Point well taken," said Tim, standing up from the boat. "I vote we get out of the blizzard. We can pay for room service later."

"But it's somebody's property," Kimberly insisted. "We can't just barge in without permission."

"Kimberly," said Jonathan, "we've just had our plane shot down and crashed. We're not interlopers. This is an emergency."

"Yeah," added Tim, "and if we died, they'd have to bury us and then we wouldn't be able to pay the rent."

"Point well made," said Robert.

"Point well taken," said Tim.

"What's this point stuff?" said Kimberly. "Since when did you guys become lawyers?"

"Yesterday," said Tim, "remember when you said you were going to have Mom and Dad lay down the law for me. So, I decided to become a lawyer. Good thinking, huh?"

"Lousy," Kimberly replied with a slight smile, "but let's see if we can get this place warmed up."

As the cousins examined the room, they could hear the wind howling outside. "Thank goodness we're not still out in that," said Lindy.

The cousins checked their phones; to their dismay, there was no reception.

"Jonathan, let's get that wood stove going," said Robert.

The two youths looked the stove over to make sure it was safe to use. Meanwhile, Lindy checked out the boat, Tim retrieved and ate a granola bar from his backpack, and Kimberly started looking for wood.

"The stove's chimney seems to be in decent shape," said Robert.

"And there's still ashes in the stove so it must still be usable," added Jonathan.

"There's only one problem," said Robert, glancing around the room. "No wood."

"We might have to burn the boat," said Kimberly.

"Wouldn't that be trespassing or something?" said Tim.

"It's an emergency situation," Kimberly replied, her teeth chattering a little. "There's an axe over there leaning against the wall. We could use that to chop it up."

"We can't do it," said Lindy.

"Why not?" said Tim. "It's an emergency. Our lives are more important than the boat. Law number 20564-B."

"Yes, and we're going to freeze to death here if we don't do something," Kimberly said.

"We can't chop up the boat and burn it," said Lindy. "It's made of aluminum."

Robert noted that the room seemed warmer than it should

be, even though the stove had not been fired up for probably years. He walked around the room, trying to find out why. In the corner opposite the stove, he found a thick board on the floor. It felt unusually warm. Lifting an edge to peek underneath it, he discovered it to be a large hatch. "Hey, you guys," he called out, "look at this!"

Robert lifted the hatch and leaned it against the wall. As he did so, a warm gust of air bathed his face.

"What is it?" called out Lindy.

CHAPTER 3

Warmth?

The rest of the cousins quickly gathered around Robert as he shined his flashlight down into the large hole in the floor. They saw dark, stone steps leading down into the ground.

"That warm air sure feels good," said Lindy. "Where do you think it goes?"

"The dungeon," said Tim. "It's so warm down there, maybe there's a dragon or monster or something. We need some pepper."

"Tim, have you been reading scary books again?" said Kimberly. "You know how reading scary books or watching scary movies always makes you afraid of the dark."

"Only *Tom and the Sneezy Monster*," said Tim. "Tom, the boy hero, always uses pepper to make the monsters sneeze so he can get away."

"Tim, now where are we going to find some pepper around here?" replied Kimberly. "Oh, now look what you've done. You've got me mixed up in your crazy ideas."

"I've got a pepper shaker in my backpack," said Tim.

"You guys can keep talking if you want to," said Robert, stepping down onto the first step of the secret stairway. "I'm going to find out where this goes."

The rest of the cousins joined him, even Tim. The upper

part of the passage was lined with rocks set in concrete, but as the cousins continued down, they could see old pick marks in the rock walls. The passage had been hand-hewn through solid rock. Tim had his pepper shaker ready.

The stairs headed straight for fifteen feet and then turned to the right. Droplets of moisture clung to the ceiling. The deeper the cousins went, the warmer the air temperature and rock walls became. An old iron water pipe, fastened to the right wall by iron straps, followed the course. The tunnel turned right again and opened into a large room about fifteen feet by twenty feet. A thirty-inch diameter shaft was dug into the middle of the floor. It was filled with water up to about two feet from its top. The iron pipe turned down the shaft and disappeared into the water.

"It must be a water well," said Robert as he leaned over to touch the water. "It's got to be eighty degrees or more."

"Be careful not to fall in there," said Kimberly.

The cousins stayed down in the warm room for over half an hour, basking in the warmth and discussing their situation.

"I was just thinking," said Tim with a happy chuckle as they got warm. "I'm glad there aren't any monsters down here. I brought the wrong kind of pepper. For monsters, you're supposed to have jalapeño."

"And who says books don't have an influence on you," said Kimberly, her toes finally thawing.

A gurgling sound started rising from the well. First, the warm water began to lower and then it reversed and began to rise and flow into the room. The water turned cold.

The cousins dashed to the stairs to keep from getting wet as cold water rose and covered the floor of the rock room. Soon, the first step disappeared into the water, then the second, and then the third. The cousins were about to turn and run up the stairs, but the water began slurping down the well and the warm water returned. The water gushed up so fast it shot up and blasted on the ceiling above the hole. Steam gurgled with the water. The warm water stopped, followed by a geyser of cold water, quickly filling the room again. The cousins had to bound up the stairs to get out of the way. The cycle repeated itself several more times before the water stopped gurgling and the well emptied of all visible water. Steam rose sporadically from the well, but the water was gone.

For dinner that night, the cousins ate granola bars and other snacks from their carry-on packs. They had learned to keep food, water, and other things on hand not only for comfort, but out of necessity. They never knew what emergency might be happening next and they needed to be ready for it.

The cousins spent a fitful night's sleep in the stairway to keep warm. They tried several times to reach someone by phone but their phones still had no service. The storm was evidently playing havoc with communications all over Gütenberg.

The Wright cousins woke up bright and early the next morning. The sky was clear and blue, the ground was covered with several more feet of newly fallen snow. The air was cold and crisp as the cousins stepped out of the building to view their surroundings. The mountains were white. The distant trees looked like stacked marshmallows. There was a high, snow-covered conical peak to the northwest of them. Their plane had crashed to the southeast or east of where the cousins now stood, but they could see no evidence of it. Everything was covered with a thick new layer of snow. It had been cold in the night as the snow was still powdery and sparkled with ice crystals.

The cousins, remembering the breaking ice episode of the day before, didn't dare try to reach their plane. It would be too dangerous to try to cross that ice again. They had no idea of the size or shape of the lake, or the depth of it. They were alive and they wanted to keep it that way.

The youths kept the stairway hatch open to try to keep the stone building warm. The warm air had returned to the well, though the water was still nowhere to be seen.

About 9 o'clock in the morning, Jonathan finally got through to Sarina by phone. "Oh, Jonathan," said Sarina, "thank goodness it's you! Are you guys okay? Where are you? My father has had search and rescue out looking for you all night long. They couldn't find any trace of you or your plane."

"We're all okay, just a little shaken," Jonathan said. "We were shot down by two fighter jets."

Sarina's end of the phone was quiet for a moment, and then she said in a choked-up voice, "Oh Jonathan, I'm so sorry! I'm so glad you're all okay...you're all alive. I'll get help out there for you. Do you know where you are? Never mind, I'll have them track down your phone location. I'll call you back in ten minutes with the details. If you don't hear from me, call me. Wait, I might not be able to reach you. Never mind, just stay on the phone. I'll use Katrina's phone."

"Thank you," said Jonathan.

Jonathan listened as Sarina phoned around to make the arrangements. Sarina talked to her father, King Straunsee. She talked to the air force. Jonathan was impressed, for as easy going and casual as she was, Sarina was an excellent organizer.

"Okay," said Sarina, finally picking up her phone again. "I hope your phone batteries are strong. The air force is sending up an AWAC plane to coordinate efforts and a squadron of fighter jets to secure your region. I've got your parents tracking your phone so our helicopters can find you. By the way, how is your phone charge?"

"48%," said Jonathan.

"Good. Keep it on."

"Thank you for your help, Sarina," said Jonathan.

"You take care," said Sarina. "Help is on the way. We'll track down who did this to you. I love you, my special friend. Get your gear together because we're going to bring you home."

Jonathan was eighteen. He had never told a girl he loved her, except maybe his mom or his sister, but that was his own family. He had never told a girl, a girl friend, that. It was too sacred, too special, it meant too much. He just stood there, holding the phone to his ear, not saying a thing. Thoughts just flying through his head.

"Jonathan, are you okay?" Sarina asked a moment later. "Is your phone still working? Are you there?"

"Um, yes," said Jonathan. "I..." He paused a moment. "Sarina? I...love you, too, my special friend."

"Mush and smooshies," said Tim's voice from behind him.

Jonathan turned around to see Tim and the other cousins standing there. He didn't know how long they had been there, but from the smiles on their faces, they had heard at least the last part of his conversation.

"Sorry," said Kimberly, "we didn't mean to eavesdrop. We wanted to hear what you'd found out."

Jonathan felt his face turning red.

"She's a sweet, good girl," Kimberly said with a large grin. "I approve."

"Yes, she is," Jonathan replied.

"Okay, what's going on?" said Sarina over the phone.

"Everybody just heard the last part of our conversation,"

Jonathan explained, his face turning redder.

"Good!" said Sarina loudly. "And now that they're all grinning, tell them I love them, too, *even* Tim. Now you guys watch for those helicopters because they should be there soon!"

"Thank you, Sarina," said Jonathan.

"Thank your parents, too," said Sarina. "They're the ones that located your phone."

"Are they listening, too?" asked Jonathan.

"Hi, Jonathan," said Jonathan's mom, Rebecca Wright.

"Anybody else?"

"You guys are so sweet," said Aunt Connie Wright.

Great Aunt Opal chimed in, "You know, dearie, I was engaged to be married when I was eighteen, just like you. I heartily recommend it. Oh, and by the way, please make sure that Timothy has properly tied his shoelaces."

"We're not getting engaged, yet, Aunt Opal," said Jonathan. "We're just friends...um, special friends." Grinning with embarrassment, Jonathan shook his head and said, "I can't believe this. Okay, everybody close your ears so I can talk with Sarina all by myself."

"Okay," came several replies.

"Sarina," began Jonathan, "you know they're never going to let us forget about this."

"I know," Sarina replied happily with tears in her eyes, "But don't worry, neither will I."

"Um," said Tim, "are we done yet? I'm getting tired of holding my fingers in my ears."

CHAPTER 4

Arrival

Soon the Wright cousins could see the contrails of fighter jets high above them in the air. Then they could hear the *rop- rop* of three helicopters approaching. The cousins walked out into the snow and flagged them in. Two gunship helicopters and one squad carrier type. There was a large, flat area behind the building the cousins had stayed in, away from the lake. Jonathan and Robert guided the personnel helicopter to land there. When the pilot signaled it was clear, the Wright cousins grabbed their gear and ran toward it through the snow. The copilot helped them aboard. Once they were all strapped in, the helicopter took off and headed north.

As they flew, the cousins could see multiple jets running interference for them. King Straunsee and his daughter, Sarina, had made sure nothing would happen to the cousins during their return flight.

They arrived at a large, very busy air force base near the town of Kleinstattz. Aircraft were being armed for the possible war. After a quick meal, the Kleinstattz Air Force Base commander and several other military personnel interviewed the Wright cousins, particularly pilots Jonathan and Robert, about their experience during their flight and the attack. They asked about the types of aircraft involved, radio transmissions, any warnings they might have received, tactics used during the attack, weapons used, and so on. The military was also eager to recover the turboprop plane's "black box" flight recorder for the electronic information it had recorded. It could help document the unprovoked attack. That would be important, especially on the international scene.

The interviews took several hours and then, finally, the cousins were cleared to leave Kleinstattz Air Force Base. An armored, chauffeured SUV with bulletproof glass arrived to take the cousins to meet the Straunsees in a nearby town. The SUV was just about to pass through the base exit gate when word arrived at the guard post that they were needed back at the base commander's office.

"What can you tell me about where you crashed the turboprop?" asked Commander Trelland, after the cousins had all gotten seated.

"It was snowing. We crash-landed on a clear, snow-covered area on the valley floor," replied Jonathan.

"Yes," added Robert, "we stopped about thirty feet or so from a bunch of big trees."

"There was a lake nearby," said Lindy. "After our plane was bombed, the ice on the lake started cracking. We barely made it to the stone buildings. We almost fell into the lake."

"And it was really, really cold," said Tim. "Kimberly's lips were turning blue."

"Thank you, Tim," mumbled Kimberly. "I don't think he needed to know that."

"Interesting," said Commander Trelland. "And how far would you estimate the crash site was from the buildings where you stayed overnight?"

"Maybe two-hundred yards or so," Jonathan guesstimated. "It was hard to tell. The snow was falling really hard as we crossed the ice."

"About 185 meters," added Kimberly, doing the math. "Why do you ask?"

The commander looked at each of the cousins. "You seem like nice kids," he said. "Be honest with me, how did you get into that valley?"

"In the turboprop plane," said Jonathan and Robert at the same time. "We had been directed to fly it to Kalisbehr by the officer at the other air force base."

"We have been looking into your story," said Commander Trelland. "No one on the base had authorized you to fly the plane. There were no control tower clearances for takeoff given and no flight plan. Please, tell me the truth now."

The youths' faces started turning red with embarrassment.

"We are telling you the truth," Jonathan said. "If you want proof, the airplane is there where we left it. It was bombed, but they weren't direct hits. The fuselage and tail were still there after the bombing. They must have straddled it."

"I wish I could believe you," said the commander, "but my personnel haven't found any evidence of the plane."

"What?!" said the cousins in shock.

"It's there," said Robert. "It's over where we told you. We're not lying!"

"Tell me, now, we don't look kindly on this kind of prank," Commander Trelland continued. "How did you get into that remote valley? By snowmobile? Were you helicopter skiing?"

The cousins looked at each other in disbelief.

"We were flying to Kalisbehr," said Jonathan. "We were caught in a blizzard. Two jets—the IFF told us they were enemies—chased us, shot a missile at us that blew our left engine apart. We crash-landed in that valley you found us in. Now I don't know why you can't see the plane, but it's there.

You look for it and you will find it."

"We have," said Commander Trelland, "with six helicopters. We've combed over every square meter of that valley. There is no plane. And besides, one of our enemy's missiles wouldn't have just damaged your engine; it would have taken the wing off your plane. A turboprop plane like that is not built to withstand that kind of attack."

"But we were using TFR," said Robert. "They couldn't get a good shot at us."

"Or they had it set on 'stun'," added Tim. "Like in space."

"Your *civilian* plane had TFR and IFF?" Commander Trelland asked incredulously, ignoring Tim's remark.

"Yes," said Robert and Jonathan at the same time.

"Those are only allowed on our military planes," said the commander.

"It's the same plane we flew from Pallin," said Jonathan.

"And what were you doing there?" asked Commander Trelland.

"Look, sir, we're telling you the truth," said Lindy. "Why are you treating us this way?"

"Because a lot of time, personnel, and resources, have been used to find you and bring you here. If you were not friends of the Straunsee family, you would be in the stockade behind bars right now. Now, how good of friends are you of the royal family?"

The interview was interrupted by a sharp knock on the door and a soldier came into the room. He handed the commander a piece of paper, which the commander read. He finally looked up. "King Straunsee wishes you to be free to go," Commander Trelland said rather reluctantly. "He's in a precarious position right now. He's taking a big gamble on setting you free, but...you may go."

"Thank you, sir," said Jonathan, standing up quickly. "Come on you guys, we need to leave."

"This won't be your last visit with me," said Commander Trelland. "Until we find your supposed plane, I'll have to keep your passports."

The cousins' jaws dropped. Giving up their passports meant they wouldn't be able to leave the country or get back into the United States. Commander Trelland would not let them go, however, until they had surrendered their passports to him. The Wright cousins reluctantly gave them to him, shouldered their backpacks, and left to go in the SUV.

"Why did he take our passports?" asked Tim.

"The possibility of war gets people on edge," said Kimberly. "People do a lot of things they normally wouldn't do. Jonathan, what are we going to do?"

"Let's get off this base and go talk to the Straunsees. Maybe we'll have to find the plane for them, I don't know."

The cousins dejectedly climbed into the armored SUV. The chauffeur drove up to the main base gate and this time received permission to leave. They were grateful to finally get off the base.

"Well," said Tim, "I guess we'll just have to get new passports."

"It's not that easy," said Kimberly. "They don't like to issue duplicate ones."

"I wish I *could* get a new passport," said Lindy, brushing her hair back. "I took a *really* bad picture."

"Me too," Kimberly agreed. "Their lighting was totally wrong."

The chauffeured drive to Twillidyr gave the cousins an opportunity to rest a while and then they started discussing their predicament. They talked quietly amongst themselves as they rode along.

"How could the plane just vanish like that?" asked Kimberly.

"Maybe somebody stole it," said Tim.

"We would have heard something," said Jonathan.

"Not if they took it out by snowmobile," said Tim.

"The air force would have seen the tracks," said Robert. "Besides, they don't make any snowmobiles big enough to take out a plane that size."

"Maybe they were space alien snowmobiles," said Tim. "They do stuff like that, you know."

"They do not," countered Kimberly, "and you know it."

"Maybe it was a big cargo helicopter that came and got it," Robert said.

"Yeah, a big space alien cargo helicopter," added Tim. "That could do it."

"You and your space aliens," said Kimberly, "Tim, I'm going to have Mom stop you from watching all those crazy space movies."

"Aw gee whiz, Kimberly, I was just teasing," said Tim, glancing up at the driver's rearview mirror. "Why does the driver keep looking at us that way?"

"Who?" asked Kimberly.

CHAPTER 5

Driven

"Our driver," whispered Tim. "I think he's spying on us."

"He's just doing his job and keeping an eye on traffic. Don't mind him," said Kimberly.

But Tim did mind. He kept watching the rearview mirror out of the corner of his eye. Each time the driver looked at he and the other cousins in the rearview mirror, Tim turned and stared back at him. The driver began to tug at his own shirt collar. Tim did the same. The driver began to sweat, Tim did the same.

"Timothy Wright, what are you doing?" called out Kimberly.

"Just sticking my tongue out at the driver," Tim replied.

"That's not nice," said Kimberly.

"He did it first," said Tim.

Kimberly glanced at the driver in the rearview mirror. The driver had a focused, nonchalant look on his face. When Kimberly looked away, the driver chuckled to himself.

"Robert," said Lindy, "you're about to lose that paper from your pocket."

"What paper?" Robert replied. He felt his pocket and a small, double-folded piece of paper fell onto the car seat beside him. He picked it up and looked it over. The handwriting was a lot neater than his. "Hey guys, listen to this," he said, reading aloud:

"**_Vital. Retrieve black box, green plane data drum, Pallin computer backup. Glasses Xlcr, Dantz._**"

"Dantz?" said Robert, looking around. "Dantzel?"

"Who?" asked Kimberly.

"She's the mystery girl Robert and I ran into at Flewdur Mall," Lindy replied. "Robert saw her again at Trifid Castle and Pallin. She left a note in Robert's pocket at Pallin, remember?"

"Yes, and she knew about the GearSpy1 clothes we used at Trifid Castle," added Robert. "I've seen her a few times from a distance with my spy sunglasses, but she always disappears before I can catch up with her."

"Maybe she's a ghost," said Tim.

"Tim," said Kimberly indignantly, "she is _not_ a ghost."

"How do you know," said Tim. "have you ever seen her?"

"No," Kimberly said. "And besides, you can't see ghosts."

"Well," said Tim, "if you've never seen a ghost and you've never seen Dantzel, then she must be a ghost. I rest my case."

"Timothy Wright," said Kimberly, "that does not make any sense and you know it."

"Hold it, hold it," said Jonathan, shaking his head with a grin. "Let's focus on the note."

"Right," said Robert, glancing back at the note. "_Black box, green plane data drum, Pallin computer backup. Glasses Xlcr, Dantz_"

"Planes have a 'black box' that records their flight data," said Jonathan. "The authorities always try to get it when a plane crashes to see why it crashed. The green plane data drum, the glasses Xlcr, I don't know what they are."

"The Pallin computer backup," Robert remembered, "it's

on the plane, too. We forgot to give it to King Straunsee."

"Maybe all of it's in the plane," said Lindy.

"Kreppen—that guy that's trying to take over Gütenberg—wants that computer information really bad," said Robert. "Slagg said he would help overthrow King Straunsee and make Kreppen king if Kreppen gave him the Straunsee Aerospace Works hi-lift rocket engine designs."

"We can't let Kreppen get that computer stuff," said Tim. "That guy's a total creep."

"We've got to get it first and get it back to the Straunsees," said Jonathan. "It's the least we can do for Sarina and her family after all they've done for us. Kreppen's a threat to all of us, to all the decent people in Gütenberg."

The rest of the cousins agreed.

Unable to figure out exactly what "data drum" and "Xlcr" meant, the cousins spent the rest of the car ride making plans about returning to the crashed turboprop plane site.

"The thing I don't understand," said Jonathan, "is why couldn't the air force find our crashed plane?"

"Don't worry," said Robert with a smile, glancing at his twin sister. "We've got our secret weapon. We've got Lindy and her photographic memory. We'll find it. Lindy, you saw where we landed, right?"

"Yes," smiled Lindy, closing her eyes for a moment to see the location. "Rocks, trees, half sunken wooden boat and all."

"Wooden boat?" asked Robert.

"Yes," said Lindy. "It was stuck in the ice near the first boulder."

"Pirates," said Tim with his classic response.

The SUV chauffeur took them to a residence of the Straunsee family called "Alpenhaus". The Wright cousins had never seen it before. The Straunsees stayed at Alpenhaus when they were needing to be nearer Alpenglow, the capitol of Gütenberg. It was on the outskirts of the city and gave King Straunsee a place to get away from the grueling demands of leading the country. A tall security wall surrounded the well-manicured grounds and the two-story Straunsee residence. As they drove up to the complex, large wrought iron gates swung open, permitting them to enter.

The driver drove up to the front of the large house and parked under the porte cochère—the overhead roof extending from the front of the house and over the driveway—which kept the snow from falling on them. As the Wright cousins retrieved their bags from the SUV, the front door of the house opened and a man stepped out to greet the cousins. He wore the uniform of a butler. "You are the Wrights, I presume," said the man.

"Yes," said Jonathan. "We're here to visit the Straunsees."

"Please come in," said the butler.

The Wright cousins, carrying their backpacks, stepped into the entry. The butler closed the door after them and led them to a large greeting area. "Please be seated," said the butler, motioning toward some plush, red velvet chairs.

"Thank you," said Jonathan and the other cousins. The cousins looked around them. A gold and crystal chandelier hung over the middle of the room; its prisms cast beautiful, miniature rainbows upon the walls, ceiling, and floor. Gold-framed paintings of majestic mountain landscapes hung on the walls. Engraved nameplates identified the scenery and the painters. There were also paintings of several of the Straunsee family ancestors. Kings and queens, princesses and princes.

Eighteen-year-old Jonathan was in awe. He had always been the natural leader of the Wright cousins and had helped in their adventures. Ever since Jonathan had met Sarina at Fort

Courage, they had been fast friends. Sarina was a nice, modest, kind, sweet and fun seventeen-year-old young woman. The Wrights had stayed with Sarina's family at Straunsee castle. It had been a wonderful adventure and a lot of fun. But sitting here in this gilded room, it hit home just who the Straunsees were. Sarina's father was the king of Gütenberg. The leader. The commander-in-chief of its armed forces. And Sarina was his daughter. Sarina was a princess. Jonathan was a commoner, a young man of no rank or position. And yet....

Jonathan continued to look around the ornate room. It spoke of authority, of power, of tradition and ancient history. Jonathan thought of his own family. He knew who his grandparents were, and some of his extended family, but that was about it. He remembered his great-great Grandpa Jake, the gold miner, but there were a lot of other ancestors he did not even know the names of. All around him, Jonathan could see the dramatic history of Sarina's family. He made a mental note to learn more about his own family history, his ancestors and their stories. Somehow, he knew that would help him keep life more in perspective.

Jonathan and Sarina's family circumstances and responsibilities were so different, and yet, somehow, Sarina, a princess of Gütenberg, possible heir to the throne, took notice of Jonathan. Why did she do that? Why did she befriend him? And yet, she did.

Whatever the future held, Jonathan and Sarina were true friends, and maybe more. Their friendship was growing dearer to each of them with each passing day. They were better people because of it.

The butler reentered the room. "I will show you in now," he said. "Please follow me."

CHAPTER 6

Return

The butler ushered the youths into a library room. The library walls were lined with bookshelves filled with books old and new. An elderly gentleman, his back turned toward them, was studying an old topographic map through the lens of a magnifying glass. The butler excused himself and left the room by the same door they had entered.

The elderly man in the library turned to greet them. The youths were surprised to see it was Mr. Gervar.

"It's the octogenarian guy," Tim elbowed and whispered to Kimberly.

The Wright cousins had first met Mr. Gervar at Straunsee Castle while they were searching for the Sword of Sutherlee. He had flown them in the helicopter to Pallin during the evacuation from Trifid.

Mr. Gervar stood and eagerly shook hands with each of the Wright cousins. "Your timing could not have been more perfect," he said. "The Straunsees are away, but Alexander—King Straunsee—has put me in charge of retrieving the Pallin computer data. If you want to help the Straunsees, this is your opportunity. We need your help in finding your missing plane. It contained some very vital information. We must return you to that valley to help us find it."

"Thank you for believing us about the plane," said Jonathan. "We were beginning to think everybody was crazy around here."

"You're the Wright cousins," said Mr. Gervar. "And I have learned that you always tell the truth."

The cousins nodded gratefully in reply.

Mr. Gervar smiled. "Will you help us?"

"Of course, yes," said the five cousins.

"Thank you," said Mr. Gervar, leading them over to look at the map he had been viewing on the desk. "The area you were in is an old volcanic region," he continued. "Thousands of years ago, it held several active volcanoes. The area is now mostly known for its health-promoting hot springs. The water has a wonderful balance of minerals. When I was a youngster, my family used to visit there often. One place," he said, pointing to a mark on the map, "was known as Cascade Springs. We could swim in the warm water there in the dead of winter, with snow all around, and not get cold."

Kimberly noticed that Mr. Gervar kept tapping his finger on the map as he spoke. She nonchalantly leaned over to see what his finger was pointing to. On the old map was a series of double dashed, medium blue lines which headed in a southeasterly direction from a cluster of several, tiny black squares with one black "L" shape in the middle of them. As she looked more closely, there were several more of the dashed blue lines throughout the valley. The double blue lines seemed to be radiating from a conical shaped mountain to the northwest of the black objects.

"There are fifteen lakes in that valley system alone," Mr. Gervar was saying. "King Straunsee sent me the air force search and rescue report on your recent rescue. You'll start your search where they picked you up. For tonight, you will find rooms prepared for you at the top of the main stairway in the guest wing. You will leave by helicopter at seven in the morning. Thank you for your help and have a good rest."

As the Wright cousins turned to leave, the library door creaked. Tim saw a shadow move at the bottom of the door. He rushed forward to open the door to see who it was. It was heavier than he thought it would be and by the time he got it open, there was nobody to be seen.

"Thank you, Tim," said Kimberly, "that was very thoughtful of you to open the door for us. There may yet be a gentleman inside you after all."

"But I..., aw, never mind," Tim replied.

As Robert stepped through the doorway, Tim whispered, "There's something going on around here. Somebody was just listening at this door."

"Did you see who it was?" Robert whispered back.

"No, but I bet it was the butler," Tim replied. "They *always* do it."

At 5AM the next morning, the cousins were awakened by a loud knock at their doors. "Time to get going," said an enthusiastic man's voice.

The cousins stumbled out of bed, rubbing the sleep out of their eyes.

"I thought we were supposed to get up at 6," Tim complained.

"They must need us to get out there sooner," said Jonathan.

The cousins ate a quick breakfast in the limousine as they were driven to the airport. A helicopter was waiting for them, all warmed up and ready to go. "Welcome aboard," said the pilot. "Please get seated. We've got to hurry and get you out there."

"What's going on?" asked Jonathan.

"Let's just say we've gotten word that there are other groups looking for your airplane," replied the pilot. "The Straunsees are counting on you."

"Okay," said Jonathan, "let's go."

The cousins quickly strapped themselves in. Jonathan noted some equipment stowed in the back of the helicopter cabin: rope, backpacks, ice picks, and other tools. The helicopter quickly lifted off the ground and headed east.

"Wow," said Kimberly, glancing out the left side window. "Look back there at the airport. There's a whole bunch of police cars there now. I wonder what happened."

"Maybe it's 'Police Appreciation Day'," said Tim.

"With flashing lights?" said Kimberly.

"Well, you know, maybe they're appreciating each other and giving each other tickets," Tim said.

"Thank you, Tim," said Kimberly, turning now to look to where they were headed.

Robert noted they were flying lower than normal. The terrain was beginning to become more rugged. Low mountains were giving way to more jagged peaks. After some time, several of the mountains looked more conical.

"Those look like volcanoes down there," said Lindy.

"Yes, this whole area was very volcanic," informed the pilot. "There are still many hot springs. This region used to be well peopled, but the eruption of 1965 made it too dangerous, and all the people moved away."

"Are we near the valley where we crashed?" asked Robert.

"According to the military charts of your journey, we are getting very close," said the pilot as they flew over a snow-covered valley. "Does anything look familiar?"

The cousins, eager to help the Straunsees, were studying

the terrain below and ahead. Heavy snow blanketed the area.

"There are the stone buildings!" Tim said excitedly a few moments later, pointing off in the distance. "We stayed in the one down there that still has the roof on it."

The pilot brought the helicopter lower, hovering above the stone building that Tim had identified.

"We were heading north, if I remember right," said Jonathan. We crashed on the east shore of the lake, somewhere over there near the base of those mountains."

"Okay," said the pilot, turning the helicopter slightly to the right and heading toward the area Jonathan had indicated. "We'll look there."

"There should be boulders and trees," added Lindy.

The pilot began flying along the east side of the valley. They made several runs, but to the cousins' surprise, they couldn't find any trees or large rocks.

CHAPTER 7

Help

Lindy closed her eyes. "They have to be there," she said, opening them again. "Large trees, boulders. There was a boat frozen in place, half sunk in the ice."

"Were you on the lake itself?" asked the pilot.

"We were near the edge of it," Lindy replied.

"Maybe the bombs set off an avalanche that buried our plane," said Robert. "When we were running from the plane toward the buildings, we were on the lake. The ice kept cracking under our feet."

"Let's fly back to the buildings. Maybe we can figure out our route from there," suggested Jonathan. "We barely made it to the ground in front of one of the roofless buildings before the ice broke up."

The pilot slowly steered the helicopter over toward the buildings. "Strange," he said as they flew, "look at that ice down there. It's all buckled. Not a smooth lake surface in sight. What did you guys do with all of the water?"

"What do you mean?" asked Jonathan.

"When the ice on a lake cracks, it usually stays pretty much in place," replied the pilot. "It floats on the water. That ice down there isn't sitting on water. It's all sunken down. Much of that ice is sitting on the bottom of the lake."

"We didn't do it," said Tim. "We were just running for our lives."

"Well, *something* drained this lake," said the pilot. "And it wasn't too long ago."

Their conversation was interrupted by a call the pilot received. He looked far to the north and said, "Okay. Anything else? Roger. Over."

The pilot looked thoughtfully at the cousins. "Tell you what," he said, "I've got to set you guys down on the ground. Maybe someplace with a better vantagepoint for you. I've been asked to help the Kleinstattz Air Force Base searchers for about fifteen minutes to shuttle some of their ground troops around."

"The Air Force?" asked Jonathan.

"Yes," replied the pilot with a smile. "You didn't think you're in on this alone, did you? King Straunsee directed Commander Trelland to find your plane at all costs."

"Commander Trelland? So, he did believe us after all," said Robert.

"But what about our passports?" asked Kimberly.

"We find the plane, we get our passports back," Lindy replied.

"I'm not privy to that information," the pilot replied. "I just do as I'm told. I'd better get you Wrights dropped off so I can go help those searching troops."

"Okay," said Jonathan. "We appreciate the ride."

The pilot nodded and headed to the north of the lake. As he did so, the cousins continued to scan the area. North and south, the cousins could see small white objects moving; Commander Trelland's soldiers in snow camouflage searching for the lost plane.

"Wow, that plane must be pretty important," said Tim, still glancing out of the window next to him.

"Let's just say our enemies would love to get their hands on it," replied the pilot.

Kimberly looked out the left window and spotted more stone structures below. Most were square but there was one L-shaped building amongst them.

"You'll notice that there are a lot of abandoned stone buildings around here," said the pilot, noting the cousins' interest. "Stone is the only thing that holds up to the harsh winter environment."

North of the lake was another group of stone buildings. They were surrounded by white tents and were next to another frozen over lake. There were soldiers scurrying around them and a tall antenna near one of the tents. The cousins could also see several white snowmobiles and a white snowcat.

"I'll get you as close as I can to the top of that tall hill down there," the pilot said. "That should give you a good view of the valley."

"Mind if we take some rope?" asked Jonathan as the pilot prepared to land. "It's really slippery down there and the rope might help us get around more safely."

"Sure," said the pilot. "And take some of that food and other gear, too. I might get stuck shuttling personnel for quite a while. I don't want you guys to get hungry or cold. There's a pack for each of you."

The helicopter whipped up a whirlwind of snow as it set down. Jonathan grabbed a large bundle of rope and handed it to Robert to carry and then grabbed a large backpack for himself.

"You're okay to get out now," directed the pilot. "Use this hand radio if you need to contact me."

"Thanks," said Jonathan, taking the radio and climbing down out of the helicopter with the other cousins as they put on their backpacks.

"If all goes well, I'll be back in about twenty minutes," said the pilot. "Let me know what you find out."

After the cousins had gotten clear, the helicopter lifted off the ground and headed farther north.

The Wright cousins adjusted the straps on their backpacks and began hiking. Jonathan broke trail through the two-foot-deep snow; the rest of the cousins followed in his footsteps.

"Boy, I'd love to have a good pair of snowshoes about now," said Robert.

When they reached the top of the small hill, the cousins retrieved their binoculars and phone cameras. They scanned to the south, trying to retrace their steps of the days before. Everything looked so different now. As they had learned from their viewing from the helicopter, their tracks had probably been erased by blowing snow.

The cousins did their best to find the place where they had leaped to higher ground as the distant lake's ice was cracking. They found what looked like the location and tried to line it up with its proximity to the old buildings. From there, they scanned the mountains to the east, searching for their crashed plane.

About twenty minutes after the helicopter had gone, the cousins spied divers in wetsuits, standing ready by the east shore. There were several troops in white camouflage coverall uniforms near them.

"Boy, they *really* do want to find that plane," said Robert, looking through his binoculars.

"I wouldn't want to go swimming in that water," said Tim. "It's freezing cold."

"You can't go anyways," Kimberly said. "Mom says stay warm."

"That's fine with me," said Tim. "There's probably not any water left to dive in anyways."

Lindy scanned the area south of the divers. "There are some of the boulders," she announced.

"Are you sure?" asked Kimberly.

"Kimberly, *it's Lindy*," said Robert.

"Oh yeah, right," said Kimberly. "Well, let's call our pilot and tell him. Then we can get out of this frozen place so we all don't die from frostbite. Timothy, your skin is looking fearfully blue. We'd better get you warmed up."

"And what color sunglasses are you wearing again?" asked Tim.

"Blue," Kimberly replied. "Why?"

"I rest my case," said Tim.

"I'll report to the pilot that we found the rocks," said Jonathan, raising the small hand-held radio to his lips. He was just about to squeeze the "push-to-talk" button when Lindy grabbed his arm and said, "Stop!"

"What's wrong?" asked Jonathan, noting the concerned look on Lindy's face.

"Don't contact the pilot," Lindy said, glancing back anxiously at the telephoto picture she had just taken with her phone. "Look at this."

The rest of the cousins gathered round to view. The screen showed a white, military-type snow cat in the background. On its side, in low resolution markings, was an ominous symbol. "That's not King Straunsee's," said Lindy. "It's from Slugdovia."

"Slagg's?" said Jonathan.

"But our pilot seemed like such a nice guy," said Kimberly.

"Yes, and look at all the nice information he got out of us," Lindy replied. "Grandpa Wright says you can trap a lot more flies with honey than you can with vinegar."

"Vinegar or not, we're in deep trouble," said Robert, lowering his binoculars, "there must be at least a hundred of Slagg's snowtroops out there!"

CHAPTER 8

Tents Moment

"Yes, you *are* in deep trouble," said a woman's voice from behind the cousins. "What are you doing out here?"

The cousins turned around to see a snow parka uniformed woman, sergeant by rank, flanked by two other soldiers. They were carrying guns.

"What are you doing on Slugdovian soil?" asked the sergeant.

"Wait a minute," said Jonathan, "we were under the impression this was part of Gütenberg."

"A lot of people make that mistake," the sergeant said. "Follow me. We can help you get back to where you need to be."

The sergeant and other soldiers led the cousins down to a flat area filled with several large, white tents. It was in a different location than the tents the cousins had seen from the helicopter.

"By the way," said the woman as they walked, "I'm Sergeant Windler. What are your names?"

"I'm Jonathan," Jonathan replied.

"We're from the United States," said Tim. "We need to talk to the American embassy. We're trying to go home."

"This is an unusual place to try to do that," said the

sergeant, studying each of the youths. "I will need to see your passports."

"We don't have them," said Kimberly.

"That makes it a little harder," said Sergeant Windler. "But we will get you properly taken care of. You needn't worry."

The snowfall was increasing as the group arrived at a large, thick-walled, heated tent. Sergeant Windler escorted the cousins inside where they found several stacks of large olive drab boxes.

"You can wait here until I can make better arrangements for you," said the sergeant with a curt smile. "I will return soon."

Before she left, the sergeant clicked a quick photograph of the five cousins and said, "Please do stay here for your own safety. There has been trouble in this region and we are trying to get to the bottom of it."

The sergeant turned and left, closing the tent door behind her.

"So, Kimberly, is the sergeant vinegar or honey?" asked Tim.

"I'm not sure," Kimberly replied.

Jonathan opened the door to ask the sergeant a question and found his way blocked by two armed soldiers.

"Please stay in the tent for your own safety as you were instructed," said one of the soldiers.

"When will the sergeant be back?" asked Jonathan.

"Soon," replied the man. "Now just sit back and make yourselves comfortable. You have nothing to worry about."

The guard closed the tent door and latched it.

"How do you like that," Kimberly said, "we came all this way out here and they just stick us in this smelly old tent with these smelly green boxes. The heat does feel good, though.

Timothy, what are you doing?"

"I'm just sitting back and making myself comfortable, like the guard said," Tim replied, sitting on a folding chair near the tent doorway.

"Oh," said Kimberly, "I guess that's okay." She shrugged her shoulders and walked to the far end of the tent to stand near the heater duct.

Tim leaned back in his chair. As he did so, he could hear the soldiers outside talking quietly amongst themselves.

"The sergeant says we are not to let the kids escape," said the first guard. "They've got something to do with the plane."

"What would a bunch of kids have to do with a military shootdown?" asked the second guard.

"I don't know. You know how sergeants are."

"Yes," said the second guard, "you ask them a question and then they let you run five miles and do pushups for the privilege. If you ask me, this is just a big waste of time. Our jets finished that plane off with bombs. There wouldn't be much left after that. You remember what happened to that fighter jet they were loading with bombs and the bomb went off. They didn't even find a tail wheel from that thing."

"That's because that type of plane doesn't have a tail wheel," said the first man.

"Well, you know what I mean," the second man replied, stomping his boot in the snow. "It was totally blown up except for the black smudge on the ground. And now, to top it all off, they have us looking for computer drives in a vaporized old plane in Gütenberg. If you ask me, it's like trying to find a beetle in a spray rack."

"Don't you mean 'a needle in a haystack'?" asked the first man.

"No, the spray rack," replied the second man. "Remember,

41

that's where we found the airplane's tail wheel."

"But that type of plane doesn't have a tail wheel," the first man said.

The soldiers' conversation turned to food.

Tim quietly got up, motioned for the other cousins to join him at the other end of the tent, and told them what he had heard. "They talked like it was their planes that shot us down," Tim finished.

"That explains a whole lot," whispered Jonathan. "That's a bunch of baloney the sergeant told us about this being Slugdovia; this is Gütenberg."

"And they're after that computer data from the plane. We can't let Slagg and Kreppen get it," Robert whispered. "They'd use it to make everybody in the world their slaves."

"Yeah, but how are we going to find the plane?" asked Tim. "They've already got a gazillion soldiers looking all over to find it."

"The bombs probably caused an avalanche," said Jonathan. "But Lindy, you said you saw the boulders?"

"Do you think the plane fell into one of the bomb craters?" Lindy replied.

"Or just got blown to bits," said Tim.

Kimberly had been unusually quiet. "Lindy," she said, "last night on Mr. Gervar's topographic map, there were some dashed blue lines in this valley. What would that mean?"

Lindy thought for a second and said, "A single dash usually means a seasonal stream. A double dash could mean an underground water tunnel. Do you remember which kind they were?"

Kimberly thought for a moment and said, "I'm pretty sure they were double dash lines. But this area is volcanic. Why would there be water tunnels around here?"

"They could mean lava tubes," Lindy replied. "They're old tunnels that formed when the lava was flowing. The top lava cooled, forming a roof, but the hot lava underneath kept flowing out, leaving a tunnel when it left. Which way did the lines go?"

"East from the cone-shaped mountain. The old volcano. One of the tubes went through an L-shaped building," said Kimberly. "Just like the one we found the secret well in."

"Then the plane might be down in the lava tube," said Lindy. "That's why the well-thing acted so weirdly. Hot, then cold, and hot again, and all that water shooting up like a geyser. It must have swallowed up the lake and our plane with it."

"If we're going to find it, we've got to get out of here before that sergeant gets back," said Jonathan. "We can cut a hole in the tent wall."

"I've got a pocketknife," said Robert.

"Me too," added Tim.

The tent was ten feet wide by twenty feet long. It was insulated with multilayered walls and had an attached floor. There was snow piled up against the bottom of the walls on the outside.

Robert and Tim selected a spot in the corner farthest away from the tent door, shielded by a stack of boxes, and began cutting a hole in the wall for them to climb through.

"Hey," whispered Robert after two minutes of trying to cut, "this canvas stuff is tough. They must have Kevlar bulletproof fabric in it; it's totally dulling my blades."

"Mine was already dull," said Tim. "Maybe it will make mine sharper."

"Sorry, but I don't think it works that way," said Robert.

While Tim and Robert were cutting the wall, Kimberly

kept watch at the door and Jonathan and Lindy started going through the backpacks they had gotten from the helicopter. The cousins needed to be able to travel fast and did not want to carry anything they would not need.

Once the backpacks were lightened, Jonathan and Lindy piled them near their exit hatch, ready to be passed through when Robert and Tim were done.

Instead of a 2-foot by 3-foot door, the cousins had to settle on an eighteen-inch by 20-inch, u-shaped flap. Robert was the first to climb out, followed by Lindy.

Robert quickly slipped over to the corner of the tent and carefully peeked around it; the guards were still there.

Jonathan passed the backpacks out and Lindy slipped hers on as Tim and Kimberly climbed out. There were no windows in the tent. Jonathan switched off the lights and climbed out, too.

As the youths were hurriedly putting on their backpacks, they could hear the whine of vehicles approaching. Robert peeked around the corner of the tent and came running back. "There's a bunch of soldiers arriving on snowmobiles," he warned. "The sergeant lady's on one of them. There are at least seven soldiers and Kreppen."

"Oillee Kreppen?" whispered Jonathan. "That creep that's trying to overthrow King Straunsee and take over Gütenberg is here?"

"He will recognize us for sure. Let's get out of here," whispered Kimberly, turning to run in the other direction.

"No," whispered Jonathan, grabbing her arm. "We can't beat them that way. They'll see our tracks."

"What are we going to do then?" whispered Kimberly, near panicking. "I don't want to see that Kreppen guy again. Jonathan, he tried to kill us!"

"We'll trap them in the tent and take their snowmobiles."

"But we don't have keys," Kimberly said.

"Most old military vehicles don't use keys," said Robert. "You guys get to the snowmobiles and we'll join you once we get the door fixed."

Lindy was watching from the tent corner. The others lined up behind her.

Kreppen and the soldiers hurried over to the tent to secure the Wright cousins. Kreppen, the old president of the Gütenberg parliament, was particularly eager to capture the youths who had defeated him at Straunsee Castle. Kreppen had even left his snowmobile running.

The group rushed into the tent only to find it totally dark inside.

"Now!" motioned Lindy.

Robert and Jonathan ran for the tent door. The guards were now inside the tent, too, trying to find the lights and the Wright cousins also. Robert and Jonathan closed the tent door and yanked the supporting poles. With a *Phoomph!* the whole tent collapsed!

"How did we do that?" said Jonathan in surprise.

"Beats me," said Robert, "but I'll take it. Let's get out of here."

The youths ran for the snowmobiles and leapt aboard. Jonathan and Kimberly were on one, Robert and Lindy were on a second, and Tim manned the third.

The cousins heard a lot of angry yelling coming from the tent and also sighted a distant squad of soldiers with submachineguns rushing toward them.

"Follow me," said Jonathan, revving his snowmobile's engine.

Desperate to get away and beat Kreppen to the lost plane,

the five youths raced out across the snow, heading southwest.

Lindy hung onto her twin brother's waist for stability as they sped along. "Nobody chasing us yet," she called out to Robert.

Lindy kept glancing back and suddenly saw soldiers coming after them. "We've got about a mile on them," she called out to Robert. "There's three snowmobiles chasing us from the north. Four more coming from the east."

CHAPTER 9

Through the Snow

Jonathan had also seen the pursuers. He signaled Robert and Tim to follow him as they sped up over the bouncy terrain. The group from the east was the most concerning; they could cut off the cousins before they reached the stone buildings far to the south by the lake.

Jonathan turned west. They would have to take a more roundabout way along the side of the mountain. Their path was getting more rugged now as Jonathan led the other cousins between two low hills. Some of the snow had piled up in drifts. The cousins plowed right through the powdery snow; the denser snow acted like jumps.

Lindy glanced back again; three more snowmobiles, also driven by soldiers, had joined in the chase.

At full throttle, the snowmobile engines were whining loudly. Jonathan and Kimberly, in the lead, hit a deep snowdrift and punched through the other side. Hitting slick ice on a frozen over lake, they spun out wildly.

Jonathan desperately steered into the turn to regain control. Robert and Tim barely missed his snowmobile as they shot past on the ice. Jonathan and Kimberly finally stopped spinning, caught up with them, and retook the lead.

Grateful for the polarized goggles and ski caps they had

found in the packs, the Wright cousins pushed on. They reached the far side of the lake and bounced up the bank there. Kimberly, hanging onto Jonathan's backpack, glanced back momentarily. There were now ten snowmobiles pursuing them.

The ground sloped upward. They entered a snow-covered pine forest and had to lean side-to-side as they weaved between the trees. The pursuing snowmobiles kept after them.

Flying out of the woods, the cousins spied some snow-covered stone buildings in the distance.

"There's our buildings," Kimberly called out.

"I see them," said Jonathan, suddenly turning down onto a frozen over river.

"What are you doing?" asked Kimberly.

"Trying to ditch our tracks," Jonathan replied.

The rest of the cousins followed them. They traveled for almost half a mile, following the course of the river, and then Jonathan turned to the right and led the cousins up a snow filled ravine. Staying in the ravine, they kept out of sight as they headed toward the old buildings.

Jonathan stopped his snowmobile near the end of the ravine and switched it off. He directed the others to do the same. Then they waited in silence for their pursuers. Through the falling snow, they could hear the sounds of the soldiers' snowmobiles, but they could not see them. The sounds first seemed to be growing louder but after several seconds they grew more faint. A few more moments of anxious listening and the sounds faded off to just the whisper of the wind driving the snow.

"Okay," said Jonathan to the other cousins, "let's go find that plane."

Leaving the snowmobiles in the ravine, the cousins rushed

over to the old stone buildings. The first building had no roof and neither did the second.

The cousins spied the third building and rushed over to it. The roof was still intact. They turned the door latch and pushed hard. The door moved inward only an inch and stopped. Glancing in, the cousins saw that the building was full of snow!

"It sure filled up fast," said Robert. "There must be a window broken on the windy side."

The cousins ran to the next side of the building.

"This isn't our building," said Lindy.

"What?" said Jonathan, studying the building and then looking around. "But there were three buildings."

"Yes," said Lindy, "but they were different than these. And there's no lake nearby, either."

"You're right," said Jonathan. "Where do you think the other ones are?"

"They must be farther south," said Lindy.

The cousins quickly ran back to the ravine. As they ran, they could hear the sound of snowmobiles approaching again. In the distance, there were several gunshots.

"Jonathan, they've got guns," said Kimberly, looking northward with a worried look on her face.

"We've been in tight places before," Jonathan replied. "We Wrights are used to tackling hard things. Now hang on tight and let's get out of here!"

The cousins started their snowmobiles and drove up out of the ravine. Following their compass, they headed south as directly as they could. Along the way, they had to skirt lava outcroppings and boulders. As they came up out of yet another ravine, they turned off their machines to listen for a moment.

"So far, so good," said Jonathan and they started out again.

The cousins were rapidly crossing another flat. The snow was falling lightly again. There were still no buildings in sight.

They were almost to the other side of the flat when Lindy saw a distant helicopter heading their way. "Robert," she called out, "a helicopter's following us."

"Rats," said Robert.

The ground was getting more rugged and the cousins had to slow down to navigate it. The helicopter flew overhead, circled, and then kept over them.

"They must be showing their snowmobile troops where we are," Robert called out to Lindy.

Jonathan turned more west, trying to find cover. They had to keep moving. The cousins hit a section with deeper snow and had to skirt several large rock outcroppings. The helicopter was still dogging them.

The cousins were now making their way along the side of a tall mountain. There were large swaths of pine forests reaching toward its top. The top of the mountain was mostly bare; it rose higher than the cousins could see through the falling snow. It was part of a chain of mountains.

Jonathan led the cousins into a stand of tall, snow-ladened pines, hoping to lose the helicopter. They brushed through ice-covered branches. It was a full minute before they came out the other side. The helicopter spotted them again as they entered another large clearing.

"Go away, helicopter, you big meanie pest!" yelled Tim as they sped across the flat to reach another forested area.

The new pines were closer together. Emerging from them, they sped out into a large, barren area. The ground sloped downward toward the east, giving them a side slope as they headed south. Far down the mountain, they could see several snowmobiles racing up to intercept them.

Kimberly pointed them out to Robert; Robert nodded, so did Tim.

The helicopter pulled ahead of the cousins and swooped down in front of them, trying to cut them off. The cousins ducked as they passed underneath it. The helicopter turned and followed them, trying the tactic again. This time it was closer to the ground.

The cousins veered to the downhill side and sped around it. They were almost to another group of trees. The frozen ground suddenly broke beneath them and the cousins plunged helplessly into a deep, dark pit with big chunks of ice and snow falling in after them.

CHAPTER 10

Alpenhaus

"Andrews, what do you mean the Wright cousins are not here at Alpenhaus?" Sarina Straunsee asked their chief butler. "I was informed they were here and my sister and I have driven half the night to get here."

"I understand, Miss Straunsee, that Mr. Gervar wished for them to go on a helicopter flight," the butler replied. "They left about 7 of the clock this morning."

"What helicopter flight? Where is Mr. Gervar?" Sarina responded.

"Indisposed," said the butler. "For all I know he may well have gone with them."

"Andrews, you know he would do no such thing without telling us," Sarina replied with fire in her eyes. "Come on, Katrina, let's go find him."

Sarina and her twin sister pushed past butler Andrews and headed straight for Mr. Gervar's quarters. When they got there, they found his room disheveled, as if it had been ransacked. Butler Andrews followed them. Sarina pressed the "panic button" on her phone and was answered immediately by security. "Where is Mr. Gervar and why is his room in a shamble?" she demanded.

"We don't know, Princess, our surveillance gear has been

malfunctioning and we are just now getting it back online."

"Get everyone in security to check out Alpenhaus," said Sarina. "And where are the Wright cousins?!"

"They drove out the rear gate at 6AM," said security. "We have video on it."

"Where did they go?" asked Sarina.

"We're bringing it up on our computers now. GPS puts the vehicle they were in at the airport."

"Who has taken them there?" asked Sarina. "Stop them from leaving the airport."

"Yes, Princess," replied security. "We have found Mr. Gervar. He is in the library. He appears to be unconscious. We are sending help."

"We will be right there," Sarina replied.

Sarina and Katrina glanced at butler Andrew's indifferent face in frustration and rushed for the library. Arriving there, they found several people, including a staff doctor, leaning over an old, gray-haired man who was slumped over in a chair. His back was to the girls.

The doctor looked up and said, "He still has a pulse."

"Thank goodness," said Sarina with tears showing in her eyes. "Whoever has done this will pay for their crime."

"What crime?" asked butler Andrews from behind them. "Mr. Gervar would not tell us what we wanted."

"What did you say?" asked Sarina in alarm. "Andrews, you are a traitor, too?"

"I am a realist, Princess," replied butler Andrews. "You girls have lived the spoiled life. It is your turn to be the servant."

"After all our father has done to help you and your family," said Katrina with distaste. "You, too, are willing to trade freedom for some promised, false security?"

"You are both naïve," said the doctor. "Kreppen will follow

through with his promises. Your father no longer has the popular support."

"You lie," said Sarina. "He has the common peoples' backing. You will see. You can never get him to quit."

"He will give up the throne once he knows we have you," stated butler Andrews. "And do not try to escape, we have this compound surrounded."

The group was now almost completely encircling Sarina and Katrina. The girls gasped when they saw that the old man was not really Mr. Gervar at all, but someone dressed up to decoy them in.

Sarina snatched a sword from its rack on the wall and swung it in the butler's direction. Andrews stepped backwards, trying to get out of the way, and fell over one of the other staff members. He backward somersaulted and sprawled out on the floor. Sarina brandished the sword, forcing the others to give ground, then she and Katrina raced for the library door.

"After them!" shouted the butler, rolling over onto his side so he could get to his feet. "After them. If they get away, you shall all be punished."

Sarina and Katrina ran for the front door, only to find the way barred by two security agents.

"You shall not get away this time," hollered butler Andrews from the library doorway.

The girls turned and raced up the main entry stairway. If they could make it to Sarina's room, there was a balcony they could make their way down from and head out the front gate. Reaching Sarina's door, they found it securely locked.

"Go for my room," said Katrina. Both girls turned and ran down the wide hall to Katrina's room. Sarina tried the handle; it too was locked!

"You forget about the latch," said Katrina, ramming the

door with her shoulder and forcing it open. "That strike-plate hasn't worked for years."

The girls closed the door behind them and ran for the small window at the opposite side of the room. Sliding it open, they quickly climbed through and out onto a lower, red tiled roof, closing the window after them. The tiles were snow-covered and slippery. From their vantage point, they could see personnel searching the grounds and men posted at the compound's gateways.

The girls carefully made their way along the roof toward a far wall. A few moments later, the girls heard a helicopter approaching and ducked underneath an overhanging roof. The helicopter soon came into view. It was white with civilian markings. The craft set down on the Straunsee's heliport and six uniformed soldiers leapt down from it. They headed for the facility's large parking garage and the house. The helicopter's blades slowed. How would the girls get free?

"We'll have to force the pilot to take us out of here," said Sarina, still clutching her sword.

The identical twins carefully made their way to a tree, shinnied down it, and swiftly but quietly headed for the helicopter. To avoid being seen, they approached the copter from the right rear side. Staying low, they grasped the rear door latch, opened it, and slipped in behind the pilot. Sarina was about to raise her sword to command the pilot, when the helmeted pilot, seeing them in a rearview cargo mirror, suddenly revved the engine and took off.

Sarina and Katrina were thrown backwards. They flailed about for something to grab onto to avoid falling out the open doorway. The copter banked hard in a turn as several bullets ripped through the door they had just come through. A canteen hanging on the back wall was hit and sprayed water all over the girls.

The helicopter banked the opposite way and the open door slammed closed. The pilot leveled off the copter and beelined it for the eastern mountains.

CHAPTER 11

The Find

Meanwhile, the helicopter pursuing the Wright cousins saw them disappear into a deep hole. It hovered in mid-air to try to locate them again. As they waited, the pilot radioed to Sergeant Windler's soldiers about the snowmobiles' location.

The helicopter was hovering close to the ground, the air from its rotor blades whooshing down onto the snow beneath it. The snow began to move, causing more snow to slide. The tumbling snow soon became an avalanche. The avalanche grew bigger and wider as it went rumbling down the side of the mountain.

"Now look what you have done," said the copilot. "If you had listened to me and gained altitude, we wouldn't be in this mess."

"Tell it to the sergeant," said the pilot.

"I will," said the copilot, "well, maybe I won't."

The two pilots watched in dismay as the avalanche they had caused gained momentum and sped down the mountainside toward their snowmobiling comrades.

Sergeant Windler and the other soldiers spied the avalanche coming toward them and turned tail to try to outrun the massive wave of snow.

On the edge of the avalanche, the Wright cousins were

alive and moving but having an extremely hard time of it. They had broken through a span of icy snow, formed by a blowing, clinging drift that had "roofed" over a narrow ravine. They were stuck under the snow in a snow tunnel as they went barreling down the side of the mountain. To make matters worse, they had to dodge dangerous icicles as they went. They tried to slow down but no matter what they did, the snowmobiles only slid on the icy snow and ice beneath them.

Before the cousins realized it, they were entering a smooth-walled cave. There was still ice on the floor where a stream had frozen, but now the sidewalls and roof were made of rock, created by an ancient lava flow. It was pitch dark except for a light spot in the distance. They reached the light spot area where the rock roof was replaced with snow and careened into another pitch-black tunnel.

Then suddenly there was a solid wall of glowing snow ahead. **Wham!** Jonathan and Kim slammed into it on their snowmobile and shot out into the bright daylight. Robert, Lindy, and Tim were right behind them as they barreled down the side of the mountain on the edge of the avalanche.

The helicopter was just turning mid-air to return to its temporary base for fuel. Out of the corner of his eye, the pilot spied the cousins' progress farther down the mountain. He quickly reported it and hurried back to refuel so he could rejoin the chase.

Jonathan kept his eye out for the soldiers' snowmobiles as he led the cousins down the mountainside. He could see the avalanche in all its terrifying majesty as it rolled rock and tree down the mountain. His sister, Kimberly, held onto him all the tighter.

There were massive boulders ahead protruding from the snow. Jonathan steered a course to the left of them. He caught sight of the helicopter leaving in the distance.

"There's an ice-covered lake down there with stone buildings," Kimberly pointed out to Jonathan.

"I see it," Jonathan nodded.

Jonathan eyed the frozen lake. Then all at once he saw it; an airplane lay trapped in the ice!

Jonathan steered for the plane. He glanced to his left to see if he could find the soldiers' snowmobiles but all he could see were the white, billowing clouds of ice crystals from the avalanche.

Traveling at high speed, the cousins were nearing the foot of the mountain. There was a large outcropping to the right and left. Jonathan steered between them. He immediately realized it was a mistake and hit the brakes. Too late to stop, Jonathan and Kimberly shot over the top of a frozen waterfall and arced downward toward a frozen pond fifteen feet below. Their snowmobile hit the ice and broke through, its nose stuck halfway into the ice and water. Jonathan and Kimberly, with Kimberly still hanging onto his backpack, were catapulted over the handlebars. They landed in a pile of snow and tumbled across the ice, finally stopping in a big snowdrift. Their snowmobile was out of commission.

Robert, on the second snowmobile, saw them disappear and hit the brakes. Tim did the same. They skidded to a stop just in time.

Cutting their machines back to idle, Robert, Lindy, and Tim quickly made their way to the edge of the precipice. They spied the damaged snowmobile and were gratefully relieved to see Jonathan and Kimberly moving, making their way up the left-hand side of the ravine.

Robert cupped his hands and hollered, "We'll back up and come around to get you."

"Okay," Jonathan called back. "Thanks."

Robert, Lindy, and Tim quickly backtracked and made their way carefully out of the ravine. They soon made it down to where Jonathan and Kimberly were waiting and pulled up beside them.

"Can we take on any hitchhikers?" Robert said to Lindy.

"Oh, I suppose so," Lindy replied with a grin, glancing at their two snow-covered cousins. "Are you guys okay?"

"Just some bruises, I think," said Kimberly, rubbing her shoulder.

"Same here," said Jonathan.

"That was quite a plunge," Lindy said. "Thank goodness you guys weren't killed."

Both youths nodded. Jonathan's face brightened and he said, "I think I found the plane."

The cousins quickly regrouped on their remaining two snowmobiles. Kimberly climbed on behind Lindy and Robert. It was a tight fit, so they had to transfer Robert's backpack to Tim's snowmobile. Jonathan took over the driving of Tim's snowmobile with Tim on behind.

"Hitchhikers," grumbled Tim as they started out.

Jonathan again led the way, a little more cautiously this time.

Avalanche ice crystals were still floating in the air as the cousins sped down the mountain slope toward the plane in the frozen lake.

The cousins still had no idea where the enemy soldiers were and realized they could strike at any time. All the cousins could do was pray and keep going. They *had* to get to the plane first.

Nearing the shore of the lake, Jonathan followed it south toward the area where he had seen the plane. They shut down their snowmobiles when they arrived and scrambled over to it. Covered with snow and ice, the wings, fuselage, and tail were bent and broken. Finding the place where the door should be, they dug away at the piled snow with their gloved hands to gain access.

"Listen!" said Lindy.

The cousins stopped. They could hear the distant whine of snowmobiles approaching.

"Don't those creeps ever give up?" said Tim.

"What are we going to do?" asked Kimberly.

"We have to get the Straunsee computer data," said Robert.

"No, we have to leave right now," said Lindy. Robert was about to protest but Lindy looked him straight in the eye, twin talk. "Something's wrong, I can feel it. We have to leave *right now*."

Robert knew better than to go against his twin sister's intuition. "Lindy's right," he said, the hair beginning to stand up on the back of his neck. "We've got to get out of here!"

Without waiting for any more explanations, the five cousins turned and ran for their snowmobiles. As they did so, there were several bright flashes followed by popping sounds on the east side of the lake.

"Somebody's shooting and it's not BB guns," called out Robert as they ran.

The cousins reached their snowmobiles in record time, climbed aboard, and sped southward. They were not prepared to be a part of any battle.

The cousins were now in a wide part of the valley where the terrain was much more conducive to snowmobiling. After several minutes, they drove up to the top of a small hill to get their bearings. They were looking back toward the airplane they had just left and saw it suddenly flash and explode into flames.

"Whoa," said Tim. "I'm glad we got out of there."

"But what about the computer data?" said Kimberly.

"That wasn't our plane," Robert replied.

"What?" said Tim. "It was sure crashed like our plane."

"I saw one of the wings as we were leaving," said Robert. "That was a jet, ours was a turboprop. Thanks, Lindy, for being sensitive and getting us out of there."

"Thank you for listening to me, brother," Lindy replied. "Now we just need to find *our* plane. It must be in the lava tube."

Hurriedly looking further south, the cousins located some stone buildings that appeared more familiar. Robert gave Lindy his binoculars to check them out. "That's them," she said with a confident smile.

The cousins leapt aboard their snowmobiles and sped for the old stone buildings. As they traveled, the crack of gunfire and resulting explosions began filling the eastern sky.

The cousins spied a snowcat vehicle up ahead and steered well clear of it. As they passed around it, they found it abandoned. It had broken through the ice and gotten stuck. It bore the markings of Slagg's forces.

Jonathan signaled Robert to slow down. They were approaching a creek which fed into the lake. The creek was covered with ice but was still flowing. The ice looked iffy.

"We're going to have to jump it," Jonathan said.

"We'll go first," said Robert.

"No way," said Kimberly, who was hanging onto Lindy who was hanging onto Robert on the snowmobile.

"Follow us," said Jonathan with a grin.

"Yippee!" shouted Tim, holding on tight as Jonathan hit the throttle. Picking up speed, they hit the ice and flew across.

Once on the other side, they waited for Robert and the girls to catch up with them.

Robert revved his snowmobile. It shot forward, hit the ice, and sped across. Just as they reached the far side, the ice behind them broke loose and tumbled into the frigid water.

"Yeehaw!" shouted Robert. "one-track-drive!"

Lindy laughed with relief as they raced to catch up with Jonathan. Even Kimberly was smiling.

As the cousins drove toward the stone buildings, Lindy glanced back to see if they were being pursued. A shiny object in the distance caught her attention. "Robert," she called out, "there's a helicopter chasing us again!"

Robert glanced back momentarily to see the new threat. "It's going to be close," he called back to Lindy.

The cousins were beginning to look like frozen snowmen as they raced through the swiftly falling snow.

Jonathan saw the helicopter, too; it was bearing down on them as they neared their destination.

The cousins were getting so close. Jonathan and the others shot past the nearest stone building. They pulled up to the second building, parked under what was left of its dilapidated porch, shut off their snowmobiles, and sprinted for the L-shaped building. They had just ducked under the roof eaves when the helicopter roared overhead.

The cousins turned the door latch but found it frozen. They pounded on it with their fists and shoulders and kicked it. The door finally broke free and swung open. As the cousins slammed the door behind them, it sounded as if the helicopter was coming in for a landing.

Inside the room, the cousins found the aluminum boat and wood stove still there. They scrambled to find something to prop the door closed with. Robert found a fireplace tool and wedged it closed.

"Everybody get to the secret stairway," said Jonathan. "We'll have to camouflage it so they can't find us."

"You really think the plane is down there under the ground?" asked Kimberly with concern.

"Yes!" said Lindy, Robert, Jonathan, and Tim at the same time.

"Okay, okay," said Kimberly.

Jonathan grabbed an old tarp; Robert grabbed a short steel pipe and an old newspaper and they headed for the stairway. Was there still water in the well?

CHAPTER 12

Wild Flight

"Where are you taking us?" shouted Katrina, hanging onto one of the back seats in the helicopter flying from Alpenhaus.

"Where you are needed," the pilot replied in a young woman's voice. "Now sit down and get yourselves strapped in. The Wrights need you!"

"Who are you and how do you know the Wrights?" Sarina yelled over the high-pitched whine of the engine and roar of the rotor blades.

"My name is Dee," the pilot replied. "It is my business to know the Wrights. They saved my mother."

"Well what are you waiting for?" said Sarina. "Fly this thing!"

Sarina and Katrina quickly strapped in. As they flew, they tried to get a good look at their pilot's face, but the helmet and tinted visor she wore kept her appearance masked.

Sarina leaned over to talk into Katrina's ear and asked, "Have you ever heard of her before?"

"No," replied Katrina. "She has black hair, though. I can see it below her helmet."

Dee glanced up at the helicopter's "cargo check" rearview mirror, noting Sarina and Katrina's questioning looks. She retrieved a flight helmet from the net bag beside her seat.

"Here," she called out, "we can talk better with these. They are wired for inflight communications."

Dee passed the helmet back and then a second one. Sarina and Katrina slipped them on and adjusted them.

"Now you may ask your questions," Dee said over the earpieces in the helmets. She glanced at the avionics in front of her. "Good," she said, "so far, so good."

"Where are the Wright cousins?" asked Sarina.

"They have been transported to the valley of their plane crash," replied Dee. "They—just a minute—yes, okay, ETA twenty-two minutes. I have extracted S2 and S3. Tell them to prepare. No, you will have to take care of that. Roger. Over."

Dee was silent for a moment and then said, "Princesses, the Wrights are in terrible danger. We have no time. We are going to have to go in to extract them. There is equipment in the two smaller duffle bags behind your seats. I must instruct you in their use as we travel. First, get into the snow clothes you will find in the blue duffle bag—."

The pilot glanced back down at her control panel and saw a red warning light flashing. "Change of plans. We're going to have to take evasive action. Hold on, this might get crazy!"

Dee nosed the helicopter downward and they rapidly lost altitude. She leveled off just above the trees, popped over a ridge, and swooped down into the next valley. Glancing back through a side rear window, Sarina and Katrina could see an ominous dark shape following them.

"It appears to be a large drone," said Dee, focusing on her flying as the object mimicked their flight pattern. "We've been located."

"Who's doing it?" asked Sarina.

"Slagg and Kreppen, your father's enemies," Dee replied. She tapped a button on her flight controller. A heads-up display appeared, bracketing the drone following them and scanning it.

"No humans aboard" appeared on the display. "Take jamming action?" asked an electronic voice.

"Yes," Dee spoke into her helmet's microphone.

A small, black disk pivoted above the helicopter's rotors, tracking the drone. Energy impulses streamed from it, causing the drone's operators to lose control. The drone's momentum carried it forward, tracing out an arc as it plummeted toward the ground. But it leveled off and started following the helicopter again.

"Oh, they want to play that game, do they?" said Dee, pushing another button. "Well, we shall see about that."

The drone suddenly burst into flames and fell rapidly toward earth.

"They've been tracking us," said Dee over her headset.

Katrina was about to speak when Dee spoke up again, talking to someone over the radio.

"Yes, the drone is no longer following us," said Dee. "Okay. We will extract the Wrights. Get us some cover...will do. Roger. Over."

The Straunsee girls heard a crackle in their earphones. "Princesses, you'd better get into that snow gear," said Dee. "We're running short on time."

"Right," said Sarina, retrieving the blue bag and opening it. Inside were white snow clothes and boots. Sarina pulled them out and handed a set to Katrina. Both girls started slipping them on over their regular clothes. To get the coveralls past their waists, both girls had to unlatch their seat harnesses. The helicopter suddenly pitched and the girls were thrown from their seats, tumbling forward. Katrina's left knee slammed into the back of the pilot's seat. The nose of the helicopter suddenly rose, sending the girls rolling backwards toward their seats.

"Sorry about that," said Dee. "I wasn't expecting turbulence in this zone." She checked their position.

The helicopter continued to pitch and sway as they gained elevation, finally smoothing up in its flight. Seizing the opportunity, the twin princesses hurriedly got their coveralls up over their shoulders, zipped up the fronts, and strapped themselves into their seats. Katrina felt a sharp pain in her left leg as she put on her snow boots.

"Hang on," said Dee. "We're going in!"

CHAPTER 13

Stairs

The Wright cousins pulled open the trapdoor to the well stairway. Switching on their lights, they rushed down the stairs. Robert was the last to go. He rigged the hatch so that when they closed it, the old canvas tarp and paper would fall over on top of the trapdoor to hide it. That done, he closed the door above him and quickly joined the others.

When the cousins got to the underground well room, they found the pipe still in place, going down the round shaft, but there was no water in the hole. The cousins got down on their hands and knees and carefully looked down the shaft.

"I don't think the plane is down there. I think it got blown to bits like those soldiers said," said Kimberly as they shined their lights down the hole.

"There's only one way to find out," said Jonathan. "We'll climb down and see. We brought some rope."

"But what if we get stuck down there," said Kimberly.

"There's no water here. That probably means the lava tube is open on the downhill end," Jonathan replied.

Kimberly was about to protest but Jonathan held up his hand. "Kimberly, we told Mr. Gervar we'd help the Straunsees find the plane. There are a whole bunch of Slagg's soldiers out there. Remember, he's the creep that tried to wipe us out in space. There's no way we can let him get that technology.

Besides, this looks like our only chance to beat them to the plane. If we do have to come back out this way, we'll leave our rope tied in place, okay?"

"Tim and I should wait here," Kimberly said flatly. "It's not safe down there."

"Lava tubes are usually large and relatively smooth," said Lindy.

"And don't forget Slagg's soldiers are coming," Robert added. "That helicopter certainly saw us come into this building and radioed the troops."

"Yeah," said Tim. "And besides, we've got to help the Straunsees. They need us, Kimbo, and I've never been down in a lava tube before and this is a cool adventure!"

Just then, a gust of warm air shot up the well. "A warm, cool adventure," added Tim.

Hesitating, Kimberly glanced up the stairs and then back down the well.

"It looks like this shaft is about twenty-five feet deep," said Robert. "Jonathan and I can just go."

"I'm coming, too," said Lindy. "If we find the plane, you'll need my help digging it out."

"Me too," said Tim. "You'll need my pepper."

Jonathan grabbed hold of the metal pipe going down the shaft and shook it. It felt strong enough, so he and Robert got rope out of their back packs and started tying it onto the pipe, beginning with a clove hitch.

Once the rope was secured, the cousins all put on gloves and got ready to rappel down. Jonathan attached a small flashlight to the brim of his hat and was the first to go. He disappeared down the hole and a few seconds later there was a loud *THUNK* when he landed on the solid rock below.

"What do you see?" Robert called down from the top of the

well.

"It opens up wide down here," Jonathan's muted voice replied. "It looks like a lava tube, all right. The tunnel is roundish and must be twenty feet wide or more. It goes off in both directions. I can't see the ends."

Lindy rappelled down next, followed by Tim and Robert. Kimberly hesitated. Then she heard muffled talking and footsteps coming from the direction of the stairway. She gripped the rope firmly and started down. The noise from the stairway was growing louder.

Kimberly landed hard on the solid rock ground below. Her knees buckled and she collapsed on the ground.

"Are you okay?" asked Jonathan, helping her up.

"Yes," Kimberly replied. "I lost my grip. Jonathan, it sounds like there's a bunch of soldiers at the top of the stairs."

"Then we'd better hurry," said Jonathan quietly, glancing down the lava tube in each direction. "Which way is east? Kimberly, do you still have your compass?"

"Sure, I've got one on my key chain," Kimberly replied. She reached into her pocket but didn't find it. "I'm sure I had it. Where did it go?"

"Here it is," said Tim, picking an item up from the ground and handing it to her. "It must have fallen out when you landed."

"Thanks," said Kimberly, reaching for the compass.

"You're welcome," said Tim.

Kimberly quickly glanced down at her compass, waiting for it to stabilize. "That way," she said, pointing toward the passage to their right. "That way is east."

"Okay, let's get going," said Jonathan, leading out at a fast pace. "The sooner we find that plane, the sooner we can get out of here."

Hiking at a fast clip in the lava tube was a new adventure for the cousins. It was totally devoid of light except for the light put off by their flashlights. The solid rock walls were sparkling with moisture. The air was so humid and warm that the cousins had to unzip their heavy coats.

At first, the floor of the lava tube was smooth but after travelling about two hundred feet, they started encountering sand and rocks spread across the floor. It made for slower going.

"It's getting hotter down here, Kimberly," said Tim. "Do you think we'll run into hot lava?"

CHAPTER 14

Underground

"No," said Kimberly. "It's all extinct. You heard the helicopter pilot; they haven't had any active volcanoes around here since 1965."

"There's always hot lava under the ground," Tim said. "Did you see the smoke coming off the top of that cone-shaped mountain."

"Those were just clouds," Kimberly replied.

"I'm not so sure," said Tim.

"What are you guys talking about back there?" Robert asked.

"Hot lava," said Tim between breaths. "Do you think we could outrun it if it started chasing us?"

"Good question," Robert replied.

The cousins came to a wide puddle of steaming water and had to walk around it.

"Hot lava can move pretty fast," said Robert.

"I think we could outrun it if we ran our fastest," Tim said.

"Maybe you guys could run fast," said Kimberly, "but I've got these big, heavy hiking boots on. There's no way I could beat hot lava. I hope we don't find any."

"Kimberly, did the map say how long this lava tube is?" asked Tim.

"I didn't see the scale on the map," Kimberly replied.

"I'll ask Lindy," said Robert. He caught up with her and soon came back. "Lindy says she doesn't know about this one, but the longest lava tube ever found is over 40 miles long."

"40 miles?" said Tim, suddenly feeling very tired. "If we run into hot lava, I can't run that far. Maybe we could make a raft or something."

"Hey, maybe that's what the aluminum boat is for," said Robert. "Wait, no, it would just melt to pieces."

"Um, guys, can we change the subject, please," said Kimberly.

The cousins were now traveling through a rockier zone. The lava tube was partially plugged with sand, silt, and assorted sizes of rocks and boulders. Tim glanced back into the darkness behind them. It was pitch black at first but then he thought he saw a faint light. "Hey guys," he said, "I think there might be somebody–." Tim peered into the blackness a moment longer. "No, I guess not."

Tim turned to look for the other cousins and saw their lights moving amongst the boulders farther ahead. "Hey, you guys, wait for me!" he called out, scrambling to catch up with them.

The air was still growing moister. As the cousins climbed over a jumble of rocks the height of their shoulders, they found the passage blocked by more rocks, sand, silt, and even larger boulders. Near the ceiling of the lava tube, twenty feet above them, they could see the trunk of a tree wedged amongst the rocks; its roots dangling in the air and dripping with water.

"Wow," said Jonathan, looking at the huge mess. "This must be where the ceiling collapsed."

"What are we going to do?" asked Kimberly. "It looks like the whole lava tube is blocked. It would be too dangerous to try to dig it out."

The cousins shined their lights at the massive pile of debris before them. Noting a three-foot-wide waterfall cascading down from the ceiling on the left side, Jonathan said, "That water's not backing up into our side of the tube. Let's find out where it's going."

The cousins followed the water's route but found their way blocked by large rocks. The water could get through; the cousins could not.

After five minutes of trying, Jonathan suggested they spread out to look for another way through. They probed the nooks and crannies amongst the pile as quickly as possible.

"This may be something," Lindy called out from the right side of the tunnel near the ceiling. The cousins scrambled over to where she was shining her light. In between two boulders, there was a gap the cousins could squeeze through. Lindy went in first to explore. She came back a moment later and said, "Follow me."

One by one, the cousins slipped into the passage. It wound around several boulders. At one point, there was a small waterfall pouring from the ceiling. The water was bitterly cold. Finding no way around it, the cousins had to crawl through the falls as fast as they could to get to the other side. They shrieked despite themselves. Kimberly shrieked the loudest, Tim's was the shrillest.

Dripping wet, the cousins emerged from the boulders at the other side of the cave-in. There was rubble strewn about but the rocks no longer went clear to the ceiling. A stream of water was flowing from the base of the rock pile. The air was noticeably colder here. Rising to their feet, the cousins shined their lights around the lava tube. It was several feet larger than the previous side.

"The lake water must have gouged it out," said Lindy. "Look over there."

Lindy was pointing to the left side of the tube where a huge room had been made. As the cousins shined their lights into it, a silver glint caught their eyes.

"The plane!" said Robert excitedly.

The cousins scrambled down from the rock pile and raced for the airplane. It was jammed in tight by several large boulders and smaller rubble. When they reached it, both wings and most of the tail appeared to be missing. The body of the plane, or fuselage, though heavily dented and scraped, appeared to be mostly intact. There was a large boulder resting against the passenger door. Kimberly took several photos of the damaged airplane.

"It looks like we'll have to go in through the cockpit," said Jonathan. "Okay, Lindy, tell us what we're looking for again."

Lindy closed her eyes to picture Robert's note from Dantzel and said, "Retrieve black box, green plane data drum, Pallin computer backup. Glasses Xlcr, Dantz."

"Black box, green data drum, computer backup from Pallin, glasses," said Jonathan. "Let's get to work."

The cousins started pulling rocks away from the plane so they could get into the plane's fuselage. The airplane's windshield was totally gone. The cockpit was partially filled with sand and gravel. They dug as fast as they could, throwing out handful after handful of rubble.

"We're supposed to find the black box," Tim said to Robert. "Does that mean the flight recorder?"

"Yes, but they're not black anymore," Robert replied, throwing a large rock out of the cockpit, "they're orange."

"An orange, black box?" said Tim.

"Yes," said Lindy, who was digging nearby. "Flight Data

and Cockpit Voice Recorders are orange so they can be found more easily. They're usually in the plane's tail so they'll survive better. They're made to withstand temperatures over 1800 degrees Fahrenheit and huge impacts. Aircraft safety standards, page 25."

"How hot does hot lava get?" asked Tim.

"Up to 2200 degrees Fahrenheit," Lindy replied.

"Then we'd better get that box out of here before the hot lava comes," said Tim. "By the way, was that an orange, black box or a black, orange box we're looking for?"

"Just dig," said Kimberly, "and hurry. I want to get out of here."

The youths had to force open the cabin door. To their happy surprise, the passenger cabin beyond was not totally filled with debris. Shining their lights around the cabin, they found that several of the seats had been broken off their bases.

The cousins fanned out to search the passenger cabin. Jonathan and Kimberly headed toward the tail of the plane to find the "black box" while Robert, Lindy, and Tim started searching for the computer drive and the green plane data drum.

Robert spied the overhead locker where he had stowed the Pallin computer drive. When he got there, he found the locker door was missing. Shining his light inside he saw the compartment was empty!

CHAPTER 15

Searching

"Where is it?" said Robert, frustrated with himself for having left the important computer drive there during their crash evacuation.

"What did it look like?" asked Lindy from behind him.

"A small, boxy thing in an olive drab duffle bag," Robert replied as he, Lindy, and Tim searched the passenger compartment. "From what I remember, I put it in one of these overhead compartments."

"Just tennis shoes in this one," announced Tim, peering in a cabinet. "They aren't mine, though, because these shoelaces are still tied."

They opened more of the overhead luggage cabinets.

"Is this it?" said Lindy, retrieving a small duffle bag from a compartment and handing it to Robert.

Robert quickly opened the soaking wet bag and peered inside. "More tennis shoes?" he said, pulling one out and looking it over. "Wrong bag."

Robert, Lindy, and Tim searched all the overhead storage but found no other duffle bags.

"I must have put it somewhere else," said Robert, trying to remember.

The three youths turned their attention to the small lockers near the plane's cockpit.

"Nothing here," said Lindy.

"Nothing here either," said Tim. "Not any duffle bag or green drums. Are you sure the note said drums?"

"Yes," Lindy replied, "keep looking."

"Robert, have you got your multitool on you?" called out Jonathan from the back of the plane.

"Yes," said Robert.

"Good," said Jonathan, "we're going to have to unscrew this panel. I think the black box is behind it."

"I'll take it to him," said Lindy, retrieving the multitool from Robert. "You keep looking."

Lindy made her way to the back of the cabin and handed the multitool to Jonathan. On her return, she stubbed her toe on a dark object. "Here's something," she called out, reaching over for a dark bag behind a bent passenger seat. Retrieving it, she found it to be a small duffle bag. It was dripping wet and covered in sand. She quickly rushed forward and handed it to Robert, who opened it.

"This is it," Robert said excitedly. "Good job, twin sister."

"Now for the green drums," said Lindy with a determined smile.

Jonathan was just removing the last screw from the panel when Kimberly spoke up. "Jonathan, what's that?" she asked, pointing out one of the plane's broken windows.

"What?" said Jonathan.

"Those lights shining on the lava tube wall over there," Kimberly replied.

Jonathan stood up. As he did, he glanced at all the cousins' lights to see where they were pointing. One look out the window confirmed his fears. "Somebody else is out there."

Jonathan glanced toward the caved zone and saw light

coming from behind a boulder. He hushed his voice and said, "Everybody, get your gear. We've got to get out of here. Kimberly, keep an eye on those lights. I'm going to try to get the black box before we go."

Jonathan knelt down, pulled the panel off, and looked inside. "The black box," he said, greatly relieved. It was indeed orange in color. A few hard kicks with his right foot broke its holding bracket off the rest of the way. The box tumbled to the floor. Reaching in, he retrieved it and loaded it into his backpack. "How are you guys doing on finding those drums?" he called forward quietly.

"No drums yet," Lindy replied.

"Not even a drumstick," said Tim. "Why are we looking for drums anyways. We don't have time to play any music."

"Drum is the shape," said Robert.

"Oh, well why didn't you tell me?" said Tim. "I thought we were looking for instruments. There are a bunch of cans in that front cabinet thing over there."

Without saying another word, Lindy and Robert rushed over to the cabinet Tim was pointing to. They threw open the door and discovered six plastic, olive drab drums inside.

"Let's get them stowed in our backpacks," directed Robert.

"What about the wires attached to them?" said Lindy.

"We'll just have to pull them off," said Robert, yanking one of the drums free. The drum was about four inches in diameter and five inches tall. He handed the drums to Lindy who in turn handed them out to the other cousins to load into their backpacks.

The cousins had found the flight recorder, computer backup, and, they thought, the green drums.

"Time to go," said Jonathan.

"What about the glasses Xlcr?" said Lindy, thinking of the

last items on the note

"I don't know what that is," said Robert. "But I do know we've got to get out of here now before whoever it is that's out there finds us." Lindy nodded in agreement.

The cousins quickly climbed out of the stricken plane. Tim was the last to leave. He had positioned something on the top of the cabin door.

There was more intense light now shining around in the lava tube. The cousins could hear muffled voices above the sound of the waterfalls. For a second, they saw a man in a white snowtrooper uniform. It looked like the soldiers had just discovered a different passage through the rocks.

Kimberly froze. Lindy grabbed her arm and whispered, "Come on, Kimberly, we've got to keep up with Jonathan."

The cousins dimmed their flashlights as they headed further down the old lava tube. For now, it was their only route of escape and hopefully the end of the lava tube, wherever it was, was still open.

Rocks and rubble, strewn about the floor of the lava tube, made the going more difficult. A light shined from behind them and the cousins immediately had to drop to the ground.

"Oomph," said Robert as Tim landed on him.

"Quiet!" whispered Lindy. "Don't move."

A bright light shined in the direction of the cousins, highlighting the boulders around them. It moved to the left, and then to the right, and then stopped directly on Tim's brown backpack. A second light was moving along the side of the tunnel.

"What's that?" called out a voice.

The cousins froze, daring not to even breathe.

"Hey, look over there," said another voice. "That looks like part of a plane. I told you it would be down here. Now we'll get the bounty for sure."

From where Jonathan was laying, he could see at least eight soldiers. Each carried a menacing submachine gun.

"Don't move until they get to the plane," Jonathan whispered to the other cousins.

The soldiers quickly made their way over to the airplane. When they disappeared from view, Jonathan whispered, "Okay, get up quietly and let's get out of here."

Drawing from their many childhood games of "hide and seek", the cousins noiselessly rose to their hands and knees and then to their feet. Shielding their lights until they could barely make out the terrain, they slipped away. They were almost clear when Tim tripped on an unseen rock and fell with a loud *CRUNCH!*

"What was that?" called out a voice from back near the plane.

CHAPTER 16

Chase

The cousins dropped to the ground again. In the dim light, they could see a soldier looking their way, shining his light. "Sir, I think I heard someone," said the man. He was soon joined by a second soldier with a flashlight. Together, they shined their lights in the cousins' direction.

"I don't see anything, corporal," said the second man. "But keep your eyes looking, those kids could be somewhere around here. We can't let anybody beat us to the data."

"Yes sir," replied the corporal.

The cousins waited until the corporal was looking at the water flowing from the large cave-in zone before they moved again.

"Sorry guys," whispered Tim. "I didn't see the rock."

"Just be more careful," Kimberly whispered back.

"Let's get moving," Jonathan whispered.

The cousins quietly rose to their feet and started on their way again. They were relieved when they turned a bend in the lava tube one hundred feet further on and could no longer see any light from the soldiers.

"Okay," whispered Jonathan, "let's pick up the pace. I don't want to be around when those guys find out that we've got what they're looking for."

"Sir, somebody's been here recently," called out one of the soldiers back at the airplane. "Here are some footprints!"

The cousins didn't wait to hear any more. They shined their lights more brightly on the ground in front of them and took off running as fast as they could. They rounded another bend and found more rubble. Carefully but quickly, they picked their way through the rubble and ran on. Their packs were feeling heavier.

As they rounded another bend, the cousins could hear behind them the clang of metal being pounded. *Clang! Bang!* came the sound, echoing down the large lava tube. Then suddenly, there were a bunch of *Achoo—achoo—ACHOOs!*

"What was that?" asked Kimberly.

"My pepper for the Sneezy Monster," Tim replied.

"Good job, Tim," said Robert as they ran.

Breathing heavily, the cousins rounded another curve and then another. The lava tube was getting larger in diameter. The tube forked. The cousins paused for a second to get their bearings.

"Let's take the right fork," said Jonathan. "It looks like the bigger one and it's going downhill."

The cousins headed down the right fork; after 300 feet, it dead-ended at a large pool of water and a cave-in.

"Back to the other tunnel," said Robert.

The cousins turned around and raced back to the fork. When they arrived, they could see faint light coming down the tunnel from the direction of the plane.

"This way," called out Jonathan as he headed down the left fork. The rest of the cousins followed him. Robert paused long enough to make more footprints in a patch of sand heading into the right-hand tunnel. He erased their tracks going to the left fork and then dashed to catch up with the other cousins.

"Good going, brother," said Lindy with a smile as they ran. "I can always count on you to cover our backs."

"You mean 'tracks'," Robert replied with a grin.

After running several minutes more, the cousins had to stop to catch their breath. They found a large boulder against the left side of the tunnel and hid behind it. Jonathan and Kimberly kept a lookout while they rested.

Then they set out again, jogging this time. They were about to round another bend when a beam of light shone directly on them.

"There they are," shouted a voice. "Get them!"

The cousins didn't wait to see how many soldiers there were. They just bolted down the large, dark, dripping tunnel with their lights fully on.

"Halt!" called out one of the soldiers, his voice echoing up and down the lava tube.

"There's no way we're doing that!" said Jonathan, running briskly. "If any of you get too tired, give me your backpack so we can keep going."

The lava tube went straight for another 250 feet and then swept to the right. Rounding the bend, the cousins hit a slippery zone of smooth, water-polished rock and went sliding into the base of a small waterfall. To their surprise, the water was warm.

Soaking wet, the five cousins clambered to their feet and raced onward. They didn't care anymore whether they were making noise or not. Their race for life was on!

The cousins rounded another bend. There was an eerie glow up ahead. Was the lava tube on fire?

"Better not be hot lava," said Tim. "I'm running out of new tennis shoes."

The cousins spied some bent-up pieces of their airplane's

wings but kept on running. The light in the lava tube was getting even brighter now, blindingly bright.

They shut off their flashlights and kept running toward the light, hoping beyond hope it might be the end of the tunnel. They could hear shouting behind them.

There was a roaring sound ahead. Water, it sounded like water. The floor was getting slippery again. Rounding another bend, the cousins' feet went out from under them and they all plunged into a large, earth-warmed flowing river. They found themselves being swept rapidly down the lava tube in a three-foot-deep torrent. The water raced faster and faster. The tube grew steeper. There was no way they could stop; the floor of the tube was too smooth and they were gaining too much momentum. One bend, two bends, three. They could see brighter light up ahead, it looked like sky light. A fourth turn and they found themselves speeding toward the end of the lava tube.

The sky outside was filled with falling snow. The cousins screamed in fright as they shot over the top of a tall waterfall and plummeted thirty feet to the deep, clear blue pool of water below.

Splash, splash-splash! They plunged into the water fifteen feet deep or more. Their feet finally touched and they sprang off the smooth rock bottom. There was steam rising from the water in the frosty, cold air as Jonathan, Lindy, Kimberly, Tim, and finally Robert popped up to the surface, gasping for breath. Struggling under the weight of their packs, the cousins made their way for the shore. They knew the soldiers could arrive at any moment.

Above the roar of the waterfall, the cousins could hear the ominous sound of a large helicopter approaching. Things had just gone from bad to worse!

CHAPTER 17

Pursuit

Dee swung the helicopter over a snow-covered ridge and into a narrow ravine. "Let me know when you see the Wright cousins," she directed.

Far below, Sarina and Katrina Straunsee could see a large, steaming waterfall cascading into a bubbling blue pool. Five heads bobbed up.

"There they are," said Sarina excitedly. "I see Jonathan!"

"And there's Robert," said Katrina. "They're all there. They're swimming for the shore."

Dee brought the helicopter down and landed it on a flat space seventy-five feet from the water's edge. She turned to tell the girls to go help but she was too late: the two Straunsee girls, polarized snow goggles and all, had bolted and were already halfway to the cousins.

Nearing the steep rocky shore, Sarina and Katrina quickly but carefully made their way down to help pull the exhausted cousins from the water.

"Sarina, what would I do without you!" Jonathan said. "Enemy soldiers are chasing us."

"I'm so glad you're okay," Sarina replied with a grin, reaching for his hand, and pulling him up the slippery bank. "We've got a helicopter."

Jonathan and Sarina worked together to pull Lindy and then Kimberly from the water while Katrina helped Tim.

Katrina next went to help Robert. She was reaching for his arm when her feet slipped out from under her. As she fell, her left snow boot flew off and hit Robert in the chest. Robert caught it by reflex and dropped to his knees to regain his balance.

Without delay, Robert loosened the boot's Velcro, slipped it back onto Katrina's stocking foot, and tightened the straps. Robert noted the surprised look on Katrina's face. "I used to work in a shoe store," Robert explained with a grin.

"Thank you," said Katrina, blushing slightly. "And *I* was supposed to be helping *you.*"

"Everybody to the helicopter!" said Jonathan.

Robert helped Katrina to her feet and all the youths scrambled to the helicopter and climbed aboard.

"Hurry and get seated," called out Dee as the youths closed the door behind them. "Enemy soldiers just came over the waterfall."

The rotor blades pounded hard as Dee revved the helicopter and lifted off. The soldiers were swimming now, trying to reach the shore. Dee turned the helicopter and headed over the nearest ridge. The snowfall was increasing.

Seeing their prey getting away, one of the soldiers retrieved a waterproof radio from a parka pocket and fumbled to click it on. "Delta One, this is Delta Two. The birds have flown the roost. They must have the tech in their packs. Repeat. They must have the tech in their packs. They are in a white helicopter. Pursue at all costs."

Dee flew low and fast. She knew it was only a matter of time before they were located again by the enemy.

Katrina, Sarina, and Jonathan were in the forward seats.

Kimberly, Tim, Lindy, and Robert were in the back. Their helicopter cleared a second ridge and dropped into the valley beyond. They were flying over a snow-covered forest.

"Where are we going?" called out Jonathan.

"Base," said Dee. "Everybody hang on, this may get interesting."

The trees cleared as they crossed over another ridge and a frozen lake. It was the same lake where the cousins had crash-landed. The cousins could see through the falling snow many alarmed soldiers far below, preparing to shoot at them. A helicopter was just taking off from among them.

The cousins could now see the stone buildings they had visited earlier that day. There were several snowcats and snowmobiles parked near them.

A cone-shaped mountain loomed ahead. Dee flew to the south of it. A wide valley spread out below them. Steam was rising from several points in the valley.

A warning buzzer sounded. "Brace yourselves," called out Dee over the intercom. "We've got company."

"Who is it?" asked Jonathan.

"One of Slagg's helicopter gunships," said Dee.

"Can we outrun it?" asked Jonathan.

"We're going to try," Dee replied. "We should be okay as long as they don't have any friends ahead of us."

The warning buzzer sounded again.

"Never mind," said Dee. "They've got friends."

Full throttle, Dee took the helicopter down to the "deck", which meant flying as low as she could without hitting anything. Trees swished by just below them, the helicopter's turbulence knocking snow off their tops.

Jonathan saw the trees and looked at Sarina in alarm.

"Don't worry," Sarina replied, white knuckled, with a grin,

"she's a good pilot."

The cousins looked out a rear window. In the distance, they could barely see a sleek helicopter giving chase. It had a menacing chin cannon.

Dee flew around a mountain ahead and dropped into a new canyon veering to the right. The helicopter gunship was still following them. Dee's instruments were tracing the movements of the threats pursuing her: three helicopter gunships, and they were closing in for the kill. She tapped a button on her controller. A heads-up display appeared, bracketing the white copter pursuing them and two additional helicopters waiting in ambush just over the next mountain.

"Scan," directed Dee.

"Chain guns: 30mm type. Air-to-air missiles: 2 pods, 152 kg.," replied an electronic voice.

"Electronics?" said Dee.

"C93-2 control module, Rev-3," answered the electronic voice.

The two menacing helicopter gunships suddenly appeared over the mountains ahead. "Gütenberg helicopter LAND NOW!" commanded a voice over the radio. "LAND NOW OR WE WILL SHOOT YOU DOWN!"

Dee tapped a red button. "Software: Rev-3," appeared on her Heads-Up Display. "Critical update Rev-4 not installed."

"Good for them," said Dee. "Interrupt C93-2. Download DECOM file to 3 aircraft. Disable weapons. Vector three helicopters to nearest clearing."

"File sent," replied the computer.

"Take them out," commanded a stern voice over the radio.

Guns aimed, the two helicopter pilots squeezed their cannon triggers but nothing happened. Their joysticks suddenly stiffened and their helicopters started to turn. Dee quickly flew between the two enemy helicopters, waving as she went by.

On the verge of total victory, Slagg's forward two helicopters were giving their pilots fits as they would not respond to their controls. The helicopters flew straight upward and then headed to a wide, snow-filled meadow. Once there, the pilots discovered the third helicopter joining them from the east. The helicopters—locked into an unbreakable autopilot mode—landed in the deep snow and shut down. As their rotors wound down, three angry pilots and their copilots climbed out to find out what in the world had gone wrong with their gunships.

CHAPTER 18

Challenge

Sarina, Katrina, and the Wright cousins continued to look out the windows into the snowstorm. They got a jolt when they saw a fighter jet streak by.

"Don't worry, it's one of ours," said Dee. "They've been flying with us for a while now. They're escorting us to the base."

"What do you mean *they?*" asked Katrina.

"There's six of them," said Dee. "When your father found out what was going on, he scrambled a flight of planes to meet us."

The rest of the journey went without incident. Dee landed the helicopter at Kleinstattz Air Force Base, the base the Wright cousins had been at only the day before.

While the Straunsee girls stayed aboard the helicopter to speak with Dee for a moment, the Wright cousins climbed down onto the slushy, snow-covered tarmac to stretch their tired legs and then walked over to look at a nearby airplane tug. It was softly snowing.

"It sure feels good to be back on solid ground," said Lindy as they strode along.

"You can say that again," Kimberly said, stretching her legs. "It's nice to be out of that lava tube."

"I thought it was kind of cool," said Lindy. "My mom would love to see that one."

"Yeah, maybe," said Kimberly. "But I sure don't miss those soldiers chasing us."

"Ditto," Lindy said with a grin.

"Speaking of soldiers," said Jonathan just after they had reached the tug, "it looks like we're going to have some company."

Two jeeps rapidly pulled up near the Wright cousins and stopped. Kleinstattz Air Force Base commander, Commander Trelland, and a squad of armed soldiers climbed out of them.

"Hello, Commander Trelland, sir," said Jonathan as he and the other cousins turned to talk with them.

Commander Trelland eyed the cousins in their damp, disheveled clothing. "Quite the outfits," he said, half grinning. "My aide said you were back. Looks like you guys had a rough trip."

"Yessir," spoke up Kimberly. "But this time we've got the evidence for you about our crashed plane, sir, and we need to get our passports back from you, please, sir."

"You found the plane?" Commander Trelland said with an incredulous smile.

"Of course," said Kimberly. "I've got the pictures on my phone."

"And we got the flight recorder and the Straunsee Aerospace data, too," added Tim.

"Good job," said the commander, "I've had my soldiers searching for those items for days. Tell you what, let me take those off your hands for safe keeping and then we'll go get your passports."

"I'll get my phone," said Kimberly, anxious to be done with the whole matter.

The Wright cousins led Commander Trelland quickly over to the helicopter.

"So, where did you find the plane?" asked Commander Trelland as they walked.

"In a big lava tube way under the ground," said Tim. "It was all scrunched up."

"I'm surprised none of my soldiers ran into you," said the commander.

Arriving at the helicopter, Jonathan opened one of its doors and Kimberly climbed in. "Where's my phone?" she said in dismay. "I had it in my pack. Where are the backpacks and where are Dee and the girls?"

"I thought so," Commander Trelland replied, his smile fading, "what kind of prank are you kids trying to put over on me this time? Let me tell you this: if you do not produce the recorder and the Straunsee Aerospace Works computer data, I will have no choice but to have my soldiers put you in the guardhouse. Now, what will it be?"

"Okay," Tim whispered to Robert, "this *is* awkward. I think I'm going to just sit in the back of the helicopter while you guys get this thing figured out." He turned to climb in but there was a soldier barring his way.

"Sergeant," Commander Trelland said, "I want that Straunsee data found. These kids say the information is here. Turn this helicopter upside-down if you have to, but I want it found."

"Yes sir," saluted the sergeant. He commanded two soldiers to begin the search.

Commander Trelland turned back to face the cousins and lined them up against the side of the helicopter. "I have been told from the field that you guys have taken top secret military information from a classified plane."

"We had it but it's gone, sir," Jonathan replied. "Somebody cleaned our gear out of the helicopter."

"And you expect me to believe that?" said the commander, eyeing the five cousins. "Sergeant, take these youths to the guardhouse. I want a full interrogation of them. That was vital military information and I will not let them get away with this!"

"Really, Commander Trelland," called out a voice from behind the commander. "Picking on teenagers?"

Commander Trelland turned around to face the speaker. When he saw who it was, his manner changed drastically. "King...Straunsee...I...your majesty, I was just following your orders."

King Straunsee, standing in the newly falling snow, was flanked by two squads of soldiers. Beside him were his two daughters, Katrina, and Sarina. Dee was nowhere to be seen.

"Trelland, *come here!*" bellowed the king.

"Yes sir," said the commander, walking swiftly toward the king. They talked briefly. When Trelland returned to the cousins, his eyes were wide.

"The king said you indeed found the items needed and he has secured them," Commander Trelland said. "Also, that I am to apologize for my treatment of you Wright cousins. I...am...you see, it was like...I apologize."

"And commander," said the king, "*you are to treat the Wright cousins as if they are part of the royal family.* Let that be understood by everyone here!"

"Yes sir, Your Majesty," everybody replied.

Surprised, Sarina and Jonathan glanced at each other, grinning widely.

"And if I *ever* hear of you treating them otherwise," continued King Straunsee, "you will have to reckon with me.

Do you understand me, Commander Trelland? You are an exceptionally good military strategist but you really need to work on your interpersonal communication skills."

"Yes sir, your majesty, sir," replied the commander.

"Commander, there's also the matter of their passports," said Sarina.

"Yes, your highness, princess," nodded the commander, "I shall get them back to them shortly."

"On second thought, maybe you should burn them," said Sarina straight-faced.

"Princess?" said Commander Trelland.

"No, you'd best return them," Sarina said, glancing again at Jonathan with a smile.

Commander Trelland ushered the royal family and the Wrights to his headquarters building where he promptly returned the Wright's passports. Before leaving the base, the Straunsee princesses and the Wright cousins met with officers Stedt and Velasco for debriefing. Officer Velasco did most of the questioning. He explained that the Gütenberg military needed to know what the youths had seen and heard, the approximate number of soldiers Slagg had sent in, and how they were equipped. Lindy's photographic memory proved to be a great boon.

The door to the debriefing room swung open and in stepped the helicopter pilot that had taken the cousins out to the valley of the airplane crash. He saluted the two officers and got permission to talk with the youths.

"I just wanted to make sure you guys were okay," the pilot said.

"But we thought you were one of the bad guys," said Tim.

The pilot looked surprised and said, "I got word that you were on snowmobiles. When I finally located you, you were just getting to the stone buildings by the lake. I landed to try to extract you from the battlefield, but you had disappeared."

"That was you?" said Lindy.

"Yes, didn't you recognize my helicopter?" the pilot replied.

"Her goggles must have been foggy or something," said Robert, "and we were in a big hurry to find the plane and get out of there."

"Several of Slagg's troops approached on snowmobiles and started shooting at me, so I had to take off again and call in our ground troops."

The cousins chatted a moment more with the pilot and thanked him for his help. The pilot then excused himself and turned to leave.

"Wait a minute," said Tim, "aren't you supposed to be grilled, I mean, interrogated, too?"

"I'm a civilian," said the pilot.

"Yeah, but we're civilians, too," Tim replied. "Wait a minute, you just saluted these officers when you came in."

The pilot grinned and opened the door.

"Wait, Mr. Pilot sir, you can't get out of it that easy," whispered Tim.

The pilot grinned, pretended to tip an invisible hat at Tim, and then stepped through the doorway. The door closed after him.

"I guess he can," said Tim in surprise.

"Mr. Velasco, sir?" asked Jonathan, "we were asked to retrieve several things from the plane. "The black box—."

"It's really orange," said Tim, and then glancing at Kimberly, said, "Well, they need to know."

"Thanks, Tim, I think they already know," Kimberly replied.

The officers nodded affirmatively.

"There was also the Straunsee Aerospace data," said Robert. "We know what that is. But what were the green drums?"

The senior officer nodded to the other and said, "They flew the plane, they know how it was militarily equipped."

"The plane you flew in," began the second officer, Mr. Stedt, "was a surveillance plane. It has side-looking radar and—let us just say—many other capabilities. We have been recording incursions made by our neighboring country infringing on our sovereignty. It is evidence that we have been under attack. We need that evidence to show to the world we are not the aggressors."

"The side-looking radar," said Katrina, "was that SLAR or SAR?"

"What?" said Tim.

"Side looking real-aperture or synthetic aperture," Katrina replied.

"Good question, Katrina," said Robert.

CHAPTER 19

Family Legend

"I'm just glad I'm on your side," Tim said to Robert and Katrina.

King Straunsee checked on the status of the royal retreat, Alpenhaus. When he found it to be secure, he arranged for one of their family helicopters to take they and the Wright cousins there. A nice sit-down, relaxed dinner was planned for that evening. Emotions were ranging all over the place, for it was also going to be the Wright cousins' last night in Gütenberg. They were leaving for America in the morning.

During the flight to Alpenhaus, the youths had a chance to finally rest and talk. It was an extremely comfortable helicopter with very plush furnishings. King Straunsee spent most of the flight speaking with his advisors and military leaders by secure communications. Slagg's forces had to be removed from their invading locations and punished for their attempts to overthrow the government and put Kreppen on the throne.

As the group walked in the front door of Alpenhaus mansion, they were greeted by a new staff and butler. The previous butler and staff were now in prison for their traitorous behavior, awaiting trial. The six security team soldiers Dee had taken there by helicopter had turned the tide and made Alpenhaus safe for the royal family once again.

Security measures had been updated.

"There's Mr. Gervar, the octogenarian," whispered Tim as he elbowed Kimberly.

"Greetings," said Mr. Gervar, "I am glad to see you are all well. I am sorry I could not greet you before your helicopter flight this morning. I was called out of town."

The Straunsees, the Wright cousins, and Mr. Gervar all sat down to a wonderful meal together, "American Fare with Traditional Gütenberg Dishes": ribeye steak, delicious hamburgers for the non-steak eaters, salad, tasty onion rings, Gütenberg blackberry pie served with ice cream, and milk or water to drink.

Midway through the meal, Tim asked Kimberly a question he had been wondering about, "Kimberly, do you think the Straunsees are related to Cinderella?"

"*Cinderella* is just a pretend story," said Kimberly.

"Oh, I know all the mice and the pumpkin carriage are just made up, I think," Tim said, "but something happened today to make me think that Katrina *has to be* related to Cinderella."

"What's that?" said Kimberly.

"Well, for one thing," said Tim, "when Sarina and Katrina were helping us out of the water, Katrina's boot flew off her foot. Robert knelt down and put it back on her foot. It was totally the *Cinderella* thing."

"Are you sure?" asked Kimberly.

"It looked like it to me," said Tim. "With all my cooties experience, I'm totally a pro at noticing that type of thing. Yep, it was the Cinderella thing all right."

"Well, Tim," said Kimberly matter-of-factly, "if Robert wants to do the Cinderella thing, it's okay by me."

"Me too," agreed Lindy, who overheard their whisperings. "Robert, you did good with the boot."

Jonathan, Sarina, and Katrina were now listening in.

"Now hold on you guys," said Robert. "All I did was put her shoe back on. You wouldn't want her to have to walk around barefoot in the snow, would you? Besides, she was helping us."

"Did you kneel down when you did it?" asked Tim.

"Well, I had to so I wouldn't slip and fall down like Katrina had," said Robert.

"*Totally* Cinderella," said Tim.

Sarina grinned and Katrina started blushing.

"He was just being kind," Katrina explained. "And no, Sarina, don't you even think about that. It does *not* count toward our old family legend. He just did it once. And besides, he was just being nice."

"Sure," said Sarina with a teasing grin. "*Real* nice."

"What's this about a family legend?" asked Jonathan.

"Well," Sarina began with a smile, "legend has it that a Straunsee princess—."

"Sarina, don't you dare!" said Katrina, blushing really good now. Katrina glanced quickly at Robert and then back to Sarina. "We needn't bother the Wright cousins with that old family tale."

"It might be important to them someday," Sarina replied with a grin.

"I will tell him—them—another time," said Katrina with an embarrassed grin. She turned to Robert and said, "So, Robert, how did you like the lava tube today?"

"Lava tube?" said Robert, looking at her curiously. "Okay, yes, well, it was pretty amazing, and when we went over the waterfall, now that was *totally* fun."

"Wait a minute," said Tim. "But what about the family legend? Katrina just totally changed the subject."

"Princess privilege," said Kimberly, smiling back at him. "Besides, she's a girl."

"*Girls!*" mumbled Tim.

That night, the cousins stayed in the guest wing at Alpenhaus. The next morning dawned bright and clear. After breakfast, the Wright cousins started loading their things into the Straunsee limousine to be taken to the airport. Sarina and Katrina were helping them.

"So, Kimberly," asked Tim, "why doesn't writing paper move?"

"Why doesn't writing paper move?" said Kimberly. "Ooo, you know, I've always wondered about that."

"Really?" said Tim. "Wow, I didn't know that. It's a good thing I asked you so you could know, too."

"Tim, the paper?" said Kimberly.

"Oh, yeah," Tim replied, "writing paper doesn't move because it's *stationery*."

"Ha!" said Kimberly.

"What was that?" asked Tim, chuckling.

"Half a ha-ha," Kimberly replied. "Personally, I use a computer."

Once everything was loaded, the time to say good-bye arrived. Sarina and Katrina stepped inside Alpenhaus for a moment to fix their hair. Sarina was already getting teary-eyed. "Katrina, why must we always say good-bye? Why can't we say 'Hi, it's so wonderful to see you!' Greetings are so much better."

"I'm beginning to see what you mean," said Katrina, wiping some moisture from her eyes as well. "That Robert, he's a good guy."

"Not you too," chuckled Sarina, wiping tears from both her eyes. "Ah, my eyes are getting all red. I'm going to be such a mess!"

"The Wrights are good people," said Katrina. "Come on, sis, let's go say good-bye to our dear friends."

There were many tears all around.

"You're a good guy, Robert Wright," said Katrina Straunsee with a sweet smile as she shook Robert's hand.

"So are you," Robert replied with a grin. "I mean, well, not the guy part. You're a pretty amazing girl. And thank you for letting me help you with your snow boot."

"Anytime," said Katrina, her eyes starting to tear up again. Katrina gave him a quick hug and said good-bye.

Jonathan and Sarina, now that was a different story. Both were doomed from the start. They did not even try to shake hands, they just hugged. Hugged and bawled their eyes out.

"I'll see you again soon," Jonathan whispered in Sarina's ear. "We are sweet friends, you and I. I feel like we have known each other forever. Keep preparing for a good future...my special friend."

"I will," Sarina whispered in reply with warm tears rolling down her face. "Take good care, my special friend, and God be with you."

"That's what good-bye really means," said Jonathan. "God be with you."

"Smoosh and mushies!" said Tim. "Come on, Jonathan, we'd better get going or we'll miss the plane."

"Thank you so much for everything," called out the Wright cousins. They climbed into the Straunsee limousine, waved good-bye, and were on their way, on their way to America. The last memory, etched in Jonathan's mind as they drove away, was of Sarina and her sisters, Katrina, and Maria, waving good-bye from the porte cochère at the front of Alpenhaus. He had no idea how that would all soon change.

CHAPTER 20

The Airport

"WELCOME TO EXCELSIOR AIRPORT," said a large sign over the roadway.

"And not a moment too soon," said Kimberly. "We've got to hurry and get our luggage checked in."

Security was heavy as the cousins entered the large airport. It seemed that every space and every seat was taken.

"Why is it so busy today?" Jonathan asked one of the airline personnel.

"Haven't you heard?" said the woman. "We're on the verge of an all-out war with Slugdovia. Their country has already attacked one of the eastern sectors of Gütenberg. Most of the foreign countries have told their citizens to leave our country. All non-essential embassy personnel and families are being evacuated on specially chartered planes."

Jonathan glanced at Kimberly. "Sarina didn't say anything about that. We've got to go back and help them."

"Mom and Dad have told us to come home," Kimberly said. "You remember that phone call last night."

"Yes, but it didn't sound this serious," Jonathan said.

"Well, evidently it is," said Kimberly. "King Straunsee and his daughters will be okay."

The lines were getting thicker as the cousins waited to

board their airplane. Planes were so filled to capacity that some of the passengers' luggage would have to be flown out in the following days.

"Now I know how our ancestors must have felt at Ellis Island," said Kimberly.

"Yeah," said Tim, "but at least they had the Statue of Liberty."

"Yes," Lindy said, "but the Statue of Liberty was on a different island, Liberty Island."

The news being presented on the overhead video screens was not looking good. Reporters were showing national guard troops being called up. Military bases were on high alert and all leaves had been cancelled. The stakes were high. Gütenberg had to show that it would maintain its sovereignty. Slugdovia had to learn that it could not, with impunity, take over its neighboring country's territory.

"Oh hi, Robert," said a young woman wearing cute glasses, walking in the bustling crowd near Robert and Tim. "Imagine running in to you clear over here in Gütenberg. Have you had a nice stay?"

The girl with the shoulder-length black hair looked very familiar, but Robert could not place where he had seen her before. It seemed like they had been away from America for a long time and the girl's friendly, familiar manner kind of threw him off-balance. Was the girl on the yearbook staff in his high school back home?

"It's been fun," said Robert. "How about you?"

"Totally fun," said the girl, "Gütenberg skiing is awesome."

"Do you think there will be a war?" asked Robert, noticing the television again.

"It doesn't look good, does it," the girl replied. "I hope war can be averted. It's funny I should run in to you like this. My mom just asked me this morning how you guys were doing."

"Wow, well, tell her 'hi' for me," Robert said.

"You can tell her yourself at the family get together next week," said the young woman, smiling. "But I'll tell her for you, too."

"I think we might be in the wrong line," said Tim, tugging on Robert's elbow.

"Hi Timothy," said the young lady, reaching out to shake his hand. "It's nice to see you, too."

Tim shook her hand quickly and said, "Sorry, we have to say good-bye now. They've already opened the boarding gates and if Robert and I don't get there soon, we'll have to swim to America."

"Then you'd better be on your way," agreed the girl. "That ocean water is very cold."

"That's what I've been telling Robert," said Tim. "Come on, Robert, our line is over there."

"Hey, well, we'll see you next week, then, at the family thing," Robert said to the girl.

"See you then and have a safe flight, and don't forget your glasses," the girl replied. She disappeared into the thronging crowd.

Robert caught sight of the TV screen again. "XLCR" it said in the corner. "The note. That's what it meant," said Robert. "Glasses Xlcr—Glasses at *Excelsior*. The glasses. That was Dantzel!"

Robert stood on his tiptoes to look for her. "Tim," he said, "that was Dantzel. Why didn't you tell me? There's so much I want to ask her."

"Girls," said Tim, pushing Robert toward the loading ramp. "How many times do I have to tell you? You've got to watch out for them. And besides, you heard what that girl said:

that ocean water is *really* cold."

Once on the plane, the cousins found their seat numbers, stashed their carry-on luggage in the overhead cabinets, and sat down. Tim was sitting next to Kimberly and Lindy. Robert and Jonathan were sitting in the row across the aisle.

Tim started playing with the lights and air vents, so Kimberly suggested he should instead put on his seatbelt and get ready for takeoff.

"Kimberly, how come I always have to sit beside you on these plane rides?" asked Tim.

"Because somebody's got to make sure you survive until your twenty-first birthday."

"But I like sitting next to Robert and Jonathan better. You always turn green when we're taking off. And, well, I didn't bring a plastic bag for you this time."

"I did," said Kimberly.

"Wow, those self-reliance classes really do help. Hey, look over there," said Tim with a plotting grin, pointing across the aisle, "there are still two empty seats over by Robert and Jonathan. I'm going to go sit by them. You or Lindy can have my seat."

"You'll do no such thing, Timothy Wright," Kimberly replied. "We've had a hard enough time getting our passports back and getting onto this flight. We might get into trouble if you're not in your assigned seat."

A noise at the front passenger door of the plane signaled several last-minute arrivals. They quickly headed down the aisle toward their seats. Two of them, young women with long, dark brown hair stopped at Jonathan and Robert's row and slipped into the seats beside them. A third late arrival slid into the empty seat next to Tim. She, too, had dark brown hair. She was close to Tim's age and was wearing sunglasses. Her brown hair hung down, covering much of her face.

Tim squirmed, leaned over toward Kimberly and whispered, "Please trade seats with me. She has cooties."

"Timothy Wright, she does not," Kimberly scolded him. "Besides, the seat numbers, remember?"

Tim grimaced, but as he did so, he felt a light tap on his left shoulder. He turned to see the new passenger looking at him. She brushed her long brown bangs out of her face and whispered, "Hi, brother dear, how do you like our wigs? Father says it's too dangerous here in Gütenberg and that we girls have to go to America."

"Cooties," Tim whispered back. "Wait, Maria, is that really you?"

Maria scrunched her nose at him. "I've got 24-hour cartoons," she said, holding up her phone.

"You do?" said Tim. "Are you sure?"

"Yes. Now what about the cooties?"

Tim looked torn. "I guess cooties...can wait until we get to America," he finally said. Then he grinned. "So, which cartoons do you want to watch first?"

Mr. and Mrs. Olsen, the Straunsee's chaperones, were seated in the row behind the youths. Three rows behind the Olsens was a young woman with long black hair and wearing cute glasses. She was nonchalantly reading a book about U.S. geography. Her name was Dee: *Dee* for Dantzel.

Please Write a Review
Authors love hearing from their readers!

Please let Greg Smith know what you thought about this book by leaving a short review on Amazon or your other preferred online store. If you are under age 13, please ask an adult to help you. Your review will help other people find this fun and exciting adventure series!

To leave a review on Amazon, you can type in:
http://www.amazon.com/review/create-review?&asin=B08GLWF6S1

Thank you!

Top tip: be sure not to give away any of the story's secrets!

About the Author

Greg exploring the bottom of the mine shaft seen in the book video trailer for *The Treasure of the Lost Mine.* You can watch the book video trailers at the author's website, GregoryOSmith.com.

Gregory O. Smith loves life! All of Greg's books are family friendly. He grew up in a family of four boys that rode horses, explored Old West gold mining ghost towns, and got to help drive an army tank across the Southern California desert in search of a crashed airplane!

Hamburgers are his all-time favorite food! (Hold the tomatoes and pickles, please.) Boysenberry pie topped with homemade vanilla ice cream is a close second. His current hobby is detective-like family history research.

Greg and his wife have raised five children and he now enjoys playing with his wonderful grandkids. He has been a Junior High School teacher and lived to tell about it. He has also been a water well driller, game and toy manufacturer, army mule mechanic, gold miner, railroad engineer, and living history adventure tour guide. (Think: dressing up as a Pilgrim, General George Washington, a wily Redcoat, or a California Gold Rush miner. Way too much fun!)

Greg's design and engineering background enables him to build things people can enjoy such as obstacle courses, waterwheels and ride-on railroads. His books are also fun filled, technically accurate, and STEM—Science, Technology, Engineering, and Math—supportive.

Greg likes visiting with his readers and hearing about their favorite characters and events in the books. To see the fun video trailers for the books and learn about the latest Wright cousin adventures, please visit **GregoryOSmith.com** today!

Enjoy every exciting book by award-winning author
Gregory O. Smith

The Wright Cousin Adventures series

1 The Treasure of the Lost Mine—Meet the five Wright cousins in their first big mystery together. I mean, what could be more fun than a treasure hunt with five crazy, daring, ingenious, funny and determined teenagers, right? The adventure grows as the cousins run headlong into vanishing trains, trap doors, haunted gold mines, and surprises at every turn!

2 Desert Jeepers—The five Wright cousins are having a blast 4-wheeling in the desert as they look for a long-lost Spanish treasure ship. And who wouldn't? There's so much to see! Palm trees, hidden treasure, UFO's, vanishing stagecoaches, incredible hot sauce, missing pilots. Wait! What?!

3 The Secret of the Lost City—A mysterious map holds the key to the location of an ancient treasure city. When the Wright cousins set out on horseback to find it, they run headlong into desert flash floods, treacherous passages, and formidable foes. Saddle up for thrilling discoveries and the cousins' wacky sense of humor in this grand Western adventure!

4 The Case of the Missing Princess—The Wright cousins are helping to restore a stone fort from the American Revolution. They expect hard work, but find more—secret passages, pirates, dangerous

waterfalls, and a new girl with a fondness for swordplay. Join the cousins as they try to unravel this puzzling new mystery!

 **5   Secret Agents Don't Like Broccoli**—The spy world will never be the same! Teenage cousins Robert and Tim Wright accidentally become America's top two secret agents—the notorious KIMOSOGGY and TORONTO. Their mission: rescue the beautiful Princess Katrina Straunsee and the mysterious, all-important Straunsee attaché case. They must not fail, for the future of America is in their hands. Get set for top secret fun and adventure as the Wright cousins outsmart the entire spy world—we hope!

 **6   The Great Submarine Adventure**—The five Wright cousins have a submarine and they know how to use it! But the deeper they go, the more mysterious Lake Pinecone becomes. Something is wrecking boats on the lake and it's downright scary. Will the Wright cousins uncover the secret before they become the next victims? It's "up periscope" and "man the torpedoes" as the fun-loving Wright cousins dive into this exciting new adventure!

 **7   Take to the Skies**—The five Wright cousins are searching for a missing airplane, but someone keeps sabotaging their efforts. Then a sudden lightning storm moves in and the mountains erupt into flames. The cousins must fly into action to rescue their friends. Will their old World War 2 seaplane hold together amidst the firestorms? Join the Wright cousins in this thrilling new aerial adventure!

8 The Wright Cousins Fly Again!—Secret bases, missing airplanes, and an unsolved World War 2 mystery are keeping the Wright cousins busy. During their research, the cousins discover a sinister secret lurking deep in Lake Pinecone, far more dangerous than they ever imagined. Will all their carefully made plans be wrecked? How will they survive? You'd better have a life preserver *and* a parachute ready for this fun and exciting new adventure!

9 Reach for the Stars—3-2-1-Blastoff! The Wright cousins are out of this world and so is the fun. Join the cousins as they travel into space aboard the new Stellar Spaceplane. Enjoy zero gravity and incredible views. But what about those space aliens Tim keeps seeing? The Wrights soon discover there really is something out there and it's downright scary. The cousins must pull together, with help from family and friends back on earth, if they are to survive. Can they do it?

10 The Sword of Sutherlee—These are dangerous times in the kingdom of Gütenberg. King Straunsee and his daughters have been made prisoners in their own castle. The five Wright cousins rush in to help. With secret passages and swords in hand, the cousins must scramble to rescue their friends and the kingdom. How will they do it?

11 The Secret of Trifid Castle—A redirected airline flight leads the Wright cousins back into adventure: mysterious luggage, racing rental cars, cool spy gear, secret bunkers, and menacing foes. Lives hang in the balance. Who can they trust? Join the Wright cousins on a secret mission in this fun, daring, and exciting new adventure!

12 The Clue in the Missing Plane— A cold war is about to turn hot in the Kingdom of Gütenberg. Snowstorms, jagged mountains, enemy soldiers. Can the Wright cousins discover the top secret device before it's too late?

13 The Wright Disguise—It's the Wright Cousins' 13th adventure, so what could go wrong, Wright...write...rite...right? Uh-oh, I think we're in serious trouble!

    The Wright cousins are back in America and diving into their active life of crazy inventions, school classroom mix-ups, and paintball battles. But their visiting friends, Sarina and Katrina, run into trouble: their royal anonymity is compromised by a story gone viral. A treacherous enemy has now placed a bounty on their heads. The Wright Cousins must drop everything and spring into action. How will they save their friends?

14 The Mystery of Treasure Bay—The Wright Cousins are traveling to the beautifully lush tropical Island of Talofa. There's so much to do: boogie boarding, scuba diving, exploring, boating, and surfing. But they also encounter danger lurking in the deep ocean waters.

    With fierce storms, spooky lighthouses, sinister traps, and menacing foes, how will the Wright Cousins unravel the puzzling mysteries before them?

15 **The Secret of the Sunken Ship**— Anyone up for a dive? This fun and exciting sequel to book #14 finds the Wright cousins searching Talofa and its neighboring tropical islands for a mysterious lost treasure. Along with amazing underwater discoveries, the Wright's and their friends face confusing clues, eerie secret caves, and a desperate gang who will stop at nothing to steal the treasure out from under them. How will the Wright cousins survive the danger and surprises that await them?

Additional Books by Gregory O. Smith

The Hat, George Washington, and Me!— Part time travel, part crazy school, totally fun. "Hey Mom, there's a patriot in my cereal box!" When a mysterious package arrives in the mail with a tricorn hat and toy soldiers inside, fourteen-year-old Daniel, of course, tries on the hat. Now he's in for it because the hat won't come off and he must wear the hat to school!

Daniel suddenly finds himself up against classroom bullies, real Redcoats pounding on the schoolroom door, and his life turned upside down. Is his American history report really coming to life?

Rheebakken 2: Last Stand for Freedom—"This action-packed novel launches readers directly into the fray on the first page and does not let go until the story's conclusion."—*Riverdancer.* The freedom of the entire world is at stake, and it's up to one man to preserve that freedom—no matter the cost.

Fighter pilot Eric Brown has been tasked with the top secret mission of ferrying King Straunsee and his daughter Allesandra to safety in the United States. Unfortunately, there are many others who would choose to see the monarch destroyed rather than permitting him to secure global freedom.

This is a fast-paced, action-centered story that will appeal to teen and young adult readers who appreciate military stories with a wholesome approach.

 **Strength of the Mountains: A Wilderness Survival Adventure**—Matt and his relatives are going balloon camping. The morning arrives. The balloon is filled. An unexpected storm strikes. Matt, all alone, is swept off into the wilderness in an unfinished balloon. Totally lost, what will he find? How will he survive? Will he ever make it home again? Join Matt in this heartwarming story about wilderness survival and friendship.

 **Wright Cousin Adventures #1 Fun Cookbook ˜ 50 Favorite Desserts You'll Love to Make, Bake, Eat, and Share!** Each delicious dessert recipe includes easy-to-follow directions and author Lisa's helpful and unique, _hand-drawn illustrations._ You'll also find classic Wright Cousin humor, puzzles, secret codes, _and_ clues to Tim Wright's "Top Secret Recipe" hidden somewhere inside the cookbook. Includes Delicious Cookies, Brownies & Bars, Candy & Popcorn, Ice Cream Treats, Cakes & Sweet Breads, and Refreshingly Fun Drinks. Delight your family and friends today with a sweet surprise from the _#1 Fun Cookbook!_

Please tell your family and friends about these fun and exciting new adventures so they can enjoy them too! Help spread the word!

Sign up for the latest adventures at GregoryOSmith.com

https://gregoryosmith.com/

Made in the USA
Las Vegas, NV
24 January 2024

84773554R00080